DAUGHTE

Damian Murphy is the author of *The Academy Outside of Ingolstadt*, *Seduction of the Golden Pheasant*, and *The Exaltation of the Minotaur*, among other collections and novellas. His work has been published on the Mount Abraxas, Les Éditions de L'Oubli, and L'Homme Récent imprints of Ex Occidente Press, in Bucharest, and by Zagava Books, in Dusseldorf. He was born and lives in Seattle, Washington.

DAMIAN MURPHY

DAUGHTERS
OF
APOSTASY

THIS IS A SNUGGLY BOOK

ISBN: 978-1-943813-39-1

"The Scourge and the Sanctuary," "Permutations of the Citadel," and "A Book of Alabaster," were first published in *A Distillate of Heresy*, Ex Occidente Press/Les Éditions de L'Oubli, 2014. A somewhat shorter version of "The Salamander Angel" was first published in *Infra Noir*, edited by D.T. Ghetu, Ex Occidente Press/Les Éditions de L'Oubli, 2014. "The Music of Exile" is original to this volume. All previously published texts have been amended where necessary.

The cover design is based on a drawing by Carel Adolph Lion Cachet, in the Rijksmuseum, Amsterdam.

For Remedios Varo
who first brought my attention to a fire nefarious and insatiable,
and for Jean Cocteau who taught me how to steal it.

Contents

DAUGHTERS
OF
APOSTASY

The Scourge and the Sanctuary

River Report # 27
October 13

D EAR SEBASTIAN,

A high wind from the north has come in on the back of the river, brutally whipping the tops of the birches which gather in little clusters all up and down the riverbanks. It howls with an unholy zest along the narrow streets and byways of my town. Only the streetlights stand secure against the barrage, maintaining their vigils with the tenacity of soldiers standing firm before a hail of gunfire.

The long row of poplars which line the river are dropping their leaves like gangrenous fingers. Dark winds skirt the river and creep up into town, meandering through the cobbled streets and narrow alleys, causing the shutters on my window to clatter and bang in an unholy cacophony. I stand upon the cramped roof of my apartment at night and survey my little town. Everything is covered in a rich tapestry of leaves, leaves, leaves: orange, yellow, dull brown, black. It's all so beautiful I could damn well cry.

We've had no rain for weeks. Sooner or later the city will be drenched under the inevitable downpour. Thunder and lightning will issue forth from heaven like a holy condemnation. When the thunder is of sufficient strength the bell in the chapel of St. Salvinus vibrates in sympathy, and the entire neighborhood is suffused with its hushed, reverberating voice; a resonant chime which echoes through the empty courtyards as if it were an angel of solace amidst the atrocities of bedlam.

Not far from here, up a wide stairway and across a courtyard, stands a building topped by a little penthouse which looks as though it has fallen into a state of disrepair. The building is a solitary and neglected tenement building of dusty red brick. Through the window of the arched doorway in the front of the building can be seen a richly furnished lobby. The brickwork on the penthouse is crumbling away after years of neglect. The windows are shuttered with rotting wood covered in flaking, turquoise paint. I can just see it from the roof of my apartment. I've been watching it intently these last few days. No lights have come on in the penthouse. I suspect it's abandoned. I've become somewhat obsessed with it, and am determined to find a way inside.

Once my curiosity has been aroused, I am powerless to let it go. The star Antares was conjunct the moon at the hour of my birth. Persian astrologers considered Antares to be a royal star, one of four which rule the vault of heaven. It burns like white fire in the heart of the scorpion. Now, the moon is the most impressionable of all the wandering stars. It's said to be the gateway for all of the other celestial forces. I bear the influence of my moon-star in the soft and malleable substance of my soul. I have always felt compelled to penetrate into the very heart of the world and taste the blood that pumps therein. The penthouse on which I've set my sights has become my Kiblah, the navel of my kosmos, the axis of my mundi. I'm certain that it conceals mysteries far too enticing for me to resist for long. Expect a detailed report concerning what I find there in a week or two.

I have a new technique which I think you'll find amusing. I found a box of keys sitting on an unoccupied dock some months ago. There must be a few hundred of them, of all different shapes and sizes. These I consecrate individually under the influence of the angel Kokabiel during Mercury's day and hour, using all of the appropriate sigils, perfumes, colors, and the rest. In this I persist until the talismanic object "swells with holy force" as they say. After a day and a night have passed it is a simple matter of slipping the key under the door of whichever place I wish to find my way inside of. The spirits of Mercury are known for their craftiness; success is assured. In point of fact, I've only done this once so far. The key in question has been shoved beneath a door leading into one side of the building which houses the penthouse, accessible only through an alleyway drenched in shadow. We'll see how well my technique works.

The winds are picking up again. The Greater Dog Star shines with breathtaking splendor through my window. I feel that the city lies in the palm of my hand. The stairways which ascend between the claustrophobic houses, shops, and restaurants; the cats which skitter up and down them; the men and women who wage an endless war against the falling leaves—all of it belongs to me. As always, just as my desire to possess the world reaches its crescendo, I'm overtaken with exhaustion and am compelled to let it go; to surrender to the star-studded night sky, to the silence of one thousand sleeping souls, to the endless flow of the river outside the window of my apartment.

In a conspiracy of autonomy,
from an empire of rust and flame,
River Station South,

Theodora

＊

Dearest Sebastian,

I love to wander the streets of my town in the early morning, just before sunrise. I am beholden to no schedule. The city is wrapped in mist and fog during the wee hours and I'm greeted by the endless discord of hundreds of alarm clocks chiming all at once, each to slightly different rhythms and in slightly different tones, playing for me a discordant, melancholy song. Thousands of people are just waking up at this hour so that they can face another day of toil, while I have but to go to sleep.

By sunrise the coffee houses have begun to open. I take my place at a table by the window of some café or other. I try to find one which I haven't yet sampled. I've taken to carrying Joyce's impossible magnum opus, *Finnegans Wake*, around with me in the mornings. It's an unwieldy brick of a book, but it's not too much trouble for me to carry in my shoulder bag. I can't imagine reading the entire thing through from start to finish. Anyway, the text wraps around from the end back to the beginning, so where to start? I prefer to open the book at random and treat it as a form of bibliomancy. Let us consult the oracle now: "Hail, Heva, we hear! This is the gilder that gladdened the girl that list to the wind that lifted the leaves that folded the fruit that hung on the tree that grew in the garden a lost rael."

You'll be happy to know that I found my way inside the penthouse last night. My little trick with the key worked like a charm. I waited in a pub across the street after the sun had gone down, sipping tonic and bitters as I kept an eye on the front door of the tenement building. Three people went in and closed the door behind them. A fourth left it slightly ajar. I paid my tab and crept in after him.

The lobby of the building turned out to be somewhat of a beautiful wreck in itself. The most atrocious yellow wallpaper hung from the walls, peeling in several spots. A slight smell of must and rot wafted through the hallways as if it were some outré brand of perfume. Dim light disguised the rat droppings which lined the walls. The furniture, on the other hand, is not entirely distasteful. Perhaps I'll return and make off with one of the elaborate little benches. It would look quite fetching beneath my window. Is Mercury not the god of thieves?

In any case, I did take something from the penthouse. More on that presently.

I made my way up five flights of stairs only to find the final stairway barred by a rusty iron grate held shut with a thick padlock. Would you believe I picked it with a hairpin? Neither would I. A nice little set of lock picks allowed me entrance after a good ten minutes of meticulous work (I am not skilled in their use). The front door of the penthouse at the top of the stairs was miraculously unlocked. Imagine my surprise when I walked in to find the place fully furnished. The decor is extravagant beyond belief. The whole place was shuttered up and dark when I stepped through the doorway. I switched on a light and it came to life.

It is not by any means a large place. Two rooms and a kitchen, with a little closet harboring a toilet and bath. The main room is papered in an oriental motif. A couch with thin crimson cushions framed in black polished wood stands against a wall beneath a large, ornately framed portrait. Tall lights stand on either side of the couch, softly illuminating the room in pale shades of eggshell. A long, red lacquer table stands wedged between heavy black bookshelves along the wall opposite the couch. Ornately framed photographs are arranged upon the table, mostly black and white or silver lithographs. What appears to be a jade elephant, reaching nearly to the point above my knee, keeps watch over the apartment from beneath an alcove set into a wall. The little alcove contains two black candles set in nice silver candlesticks, between which sits a small black box containing a deck of cards that must be seen to be believed.

The four suits are indicated by figures wearing the heads of animals: tigers, falcons, antelopes and rabbits. From this I removed the Queen of Spades, decorated with an image of a woman in a long silk dress of amber enwrapped in piercing flames of jade. She has the head of an antelope, and casts a reproachful gaze over her left shoulder as if to sour the will of an unseen assailant. She holds a spade in her left hand. I simply could not resist keeping this memento for myself.

The bookshelves display a truly remarkable selection: *The Grand Grimoire, The 5th and 6th Books of Moses, The Philosophia Pnuematica, The Grimorum Verum, The Black Pullet*—these were merely the ones which I'd recognized. Alongside those, several books I'd never heard of: *The Book of the Fabulous Gryphon, Intoxication of the Night Goat, The Incantations of the Peacock Angel,* and several others. One entire shelf is dedicated to Kabbalistic works in Hebrew, another contains a nice collection of Arabic grimoires. Simply unbelievable. Sore tempted I was to lift a precious volume or six for myself, but I felt I must show some restraint.

The painting above the couch caused my breath to stop short when I first caught sight of it. In the foreground of the painting stands a woman in a black windswept dress. The expression on her face might cause an angel to convulse if one were so unfortunate as to pass before her. She stands near the lip of an overhanging ridge choked with weeds and rough shrubs, one foot extended as if she intends to stroll right off the edge and into the perilous waves which surge and break below. An intricate design depicting a circle of black bees is woven into the fabric of her dress just below the neck. Her hands are an enigma all unto themselves; every muscle is supremely tensed, all the way up to her elbows. The left hand tightly grips a long rod of black wood set with several bands of (perhaps) copper. It extends all the way down to the ground near her feet. The top of the rod opens out into a floral motif, also of copper. Her right hand extends from her side just a little, and is locked into a perilous grip as if to command the wind and rain through sheer temerity. Indeed, the winds blow fierce and savage behind her. The trees in the background are fair overwhelmed with the force of the gale, nearly torn free from their moorings in the earth. The whole scene is painted in the most sensuous fashion, the paint swirls and flows in a manner almost obscene. All of it is framed in an imposing monstrosity of heavy black wood, adorned at the corners with diabolical flourishes. The piece is so sumptuous I could almost make love to it.

The apartment is simply too rich to describe in great detail in the space of a single letter. For now I'll highlight just a few more essentials.

The bedroom houses an elaborate four-poster bed and a delightful octagonal nightstand carved from wood. Hugging the wall opposite the bed is a mahogany armoire adorned with delicate brass plates from which hang tiny brass handles. I held back from exploring the bedroom beyond just a quick glance. I feel that some things must be left alone.

The kitchen looks as if it hasn't been used in ages. Tightly packed cupboards crowd around a little stove. An immaculate black dining table occupies the far wall. Above the table hangs a quaint little chandelier which lights the place quite nicely. An elegant iron wine rack adorns the table, while a cabinet full of herbs and oils and spices hangs above. A very modest icebox, unplugged and empty, stands nestled just inside the entryway by the stove. All in all, it seems an intimate place to share a meal.

The water closet bears little mention, except for the bathtub, which rests upon clawed feet. I want one just like it, but would have to sell my body well into my elder years in order to afford one. Hexagonal tiles cover the floor, pearl with amber grout, while the walls are papered in sumptuous shades of crimson and gold.

I remained in the penthouse for quite some time, reclining on the couch, so as to absorb the devastating beauty of the place. I wished for it to leave an impression in my very bones. I really must come back. I want to peruse the library at the very least. In view of this, I retrieved my little talisman (still lying on the floor on the other side of the entrance by the alleyway) and placed it in a drawer which is set into the nightstand in the bedroom. This will ensure that I have no trouble gaining entrance in the future. I replaced the padlock on the gate when at last I left, but didn't push it closed completely in order to save myself the trouble of having to pick it again. All in all, I couldn't be more pleased. I must remember to burn some copal on the roof of my apartment as a reward for the angels of Mercury.

There are several other things besides, but I don't feel moved to write about them just yet. Maybe I'll include them in my next report. My pen grows weary and I want to take a stroll beneath the early morning moonlight before I succumb to the tyranny of sleep.

In things that ought not to be done,
from a place I ought not to have gone,
in continuous recirculation from bend of shore to swerve of bay,
River Station South,

Theodora

✳

Dear Sebastian,

Winter approaches. The city was besieged by the first faint flurries of snow just this last week. The deluge has yet to come. We ought to have at least a few days of heavy snow before the new year.

Tomorrow morning I invoke the Beni Seraphim, the sons of the winged and fiery serpents depicted in the Book of Exodus. I feel the need for a purification of sorts. I've worked with them before. They appear to my inner vision as little writhing flames. They burn away the pockets of obstinacy which build up in the personality as we take refuge from the cruelty and indifference of the world. I feel that my character has grown a little stale this past year. I wish to remain true to the essential parts of my nature, and to forget the rest.

I have a bottle of wine in my cupboard which is perfect for the rite. It was consumed by the soldiers of Eger Castle during the siege led by the Ottoman Sultan in the 16th century. The strength and vitality of the defending soldiers so astonished the Turkish invaders that there were rumors that their wine was mixed with bull's blood. The attacking Ottoman soldiers finally gave up in despair after forty days of fruitless advances on the castle. The wine should make a fine Eucharist.

The fallen leaves grow sparse along the streets of my little town; those that remain are stiff with frost. They play for me a symphony beneath my feet as I walk briskly from one icy square to another. I peer into uncovered windows and covet the contents of exposed balconies. One thousand people live within the modest rooms arranged like pieces in a jigsaw puzzle scattered throughout the town, and every single one of them has a different point of view, each with their own unique experience, each occupying their own particular space with its own particular flavors, scents, and colors. I want to experience it all, but then what would remain for me to explore, to yearn for? The soul is nourished by mystery alone. If everything were to be known then the mind would feast but the soul would starve, and life would lose its color.

I have twice now returned to the penthouse. I feel as if it has become a part of me, a hidden chamber of my incestuous heart. I have penetrated into its secret abysses and it into mine. There is a permanence about the place, as if it's left its mark on the etheric essence which stands behind and sustains the world.

Crossing over the threshold of the entrance to the penthouse a second time, I felt that I had returned to a place long familiar to me. I was compelled to submerge myself ever deeper into its subtle foundations. I sought an intimate connection, a consummation of the initial exchange between myself and the genius of the space. I removed my clothes, lay myself upon the intricate carpet beneath the lights, and gave myself without reserve to the spirit of the place. I found a perverse pleasure at the thought of the owner of the penthouse walking in to see me spread out on the carpet, naked and shameless. What a beast I am! Whatever you may think, I cannot but feel that my actions are not only justified but necessary. We each must establish our presence in the world in a way which is consistent with our nature. It just so happens that my nature is at variance with the established values of the society in which I live.

I remained so exposed for the duration of my stay, during which time I happened upon a delicious little drawer hidden behind a decorative curtain which obscures a section of the wall in the foyer. The drawer, no more than eight inches wide, pulled out to reveal an intricate map of the city. It took me little time at all to discern that the map was not quite right. Certain squares and courtyards opened up to streets that don't exist. Alleyways were found which had no physical analog, and several thoroughfares and walkaways were missing altogether. A church in the northeast was shown much further south than it should be. A mysterious fountain appeared between two stairways. There were little more than a dozen inconsistencies in all. I know this town like a mother knows her child so the anomalies weren't hard for me to locate. The differences between the map and the town which it purports to document couldn't be due to the age of the map; the topography of the land doesn't quite line up. Further, several modern structures do appear, which tells me that the map was put together fairly recently. There are no street names, nor any words at all save for the word "AVR" in red capital letters above a drawing of a chameleon.

Along with the map I found a silver matchbox (perhaps to burn the evidence?), decorated with the stylized image of a scarab beetle. I could not bring myself to open this —invasion of privacy has its limits after all. I am quite certain that the box contains something other than matches.

Lastly, I found a faded black and white photograph of an older man in military attire. He looked the very figure of the devil in his cap, boots and waistcoat. Black, beady eyes stared right through the surface of the photograph. He leaned upon a cane with an ivory handle carved into the shape of some sort of animal head. His face betrayed the calm certitude granted only to those who know too much.

I pushed the drawer back in and replaced the curtain exactly as I'd found it. Later, as I wound my way along a sinuous route back to my apartment, paying close attention to several areas in which the topography differed from that which was shown on the spurious map, I found myself immersed in meditations on secrecy and revelation. I cannot help but feel that I've left something of myself, some mark or influence, upon the things that I found inside the drawer. There is a particular set of laws which determine the impression that we leave upon a thing which we are not supposed to see. A bond between the observer and that which is observed is established, and several subtle manifestations arise therefrom. How is this relationship affected by my relating these discoveries to you, and how does it compare with those things which I choose not to reveal? I am perplexed, but only partly so.

The next evening I returned. The house seemed to embrace me, as if to signal its acceptance of the offering implicit in my actions of the night before. For the first time, I sat on that magnificent couch as a true inhabitant of the space. If I never return to this place even once in my life, it will nevertheless continue to be my home.

What else is there to say? Where the penthouse is fairly insulated, my apartment seems to be made of rice paper. At night, I wrap myself in blankets, chilled to the bone. It's quite likely I'll damn well freeze to death. If you don't hear from me for more than a couple of weeks, please send somebody straight away to dump my frigid corpse into the river.

Yet still, I love to watch the city from my roof, all bundled up and shivering, icy stars gleaming like shattered teeth on black velvet, the very constellations fixed in place like principalities in a petrified empire. The cats don't seem to give a damn about the cold. They crowd the streets looking for food, mewling up a veritable cacophony which keeps me from sleeping at night. I try to imagine the anomalies in the map superimposed over the streets as they appear before me. Purely from memory, I can spot several major differences. In my mind, I creep along the phantom alleys, bathe in the lustral waters of an invisible fountain, lie in repose upon painted benches in the nonexistent squares. I occupy spaces scarcely imagined and partake of fruits rarely tasted. There are treasures hidden in the shadows that do not appear in the clear light of day.

Let us see what a quick dip in the *Wake* reveals before I bring this letter to a close: "She'll confess it by her figure and she'll deny it to your face. She's sworn a pact and smacked in a continuous line unbrothen cross her screaming scathing back."

So there you have it.

In blood and spit and tears and semen,
from my secret enclave hidden amongst the ruins of an imaginary city,
River Station South,

Theodora

*

Theodora reclines upon a crimson cushion set into a frame of black lacquered wood. Above her hangs a painting in an ornate wooden frame depicting a voluptuous seascape assailed by high winds. A single lamp illuminates the room, casting a soft, orange glow which rests upon the furniture and the figures sitting thereon. On one side of the couch, not far from Theodora, sits a heavyset woman in a single-piece dress of iridescent gold which almost entirely covers her ample flesh. The dress is attached at the front with pearl buttons, while the cuffs are decorated with tiny embroidered bees, just visible against the fabric in the dim light. The woman is older than Theodora; one would guess that she is perhaps in the later years of her fifth decade.

Sitting in a plush red leather armchair at an opposing angle to the couch is a gentleman who appears to be just a little older than the woman. He appears quite dapper, dressed in a dark suit with black tie. A certain joviality assuages the austerity of his eyes, which are set like black and scintillating diamonds in his lined face. His mouth hangs always just a little open in a lopsided grin. He has a tendency, when enthused, to grip the ivory handle of a silver cane which rests against a knee. His other hand elevates a tiny glass of scotch before him.

"You've managed to penetrate into the inmost chambers of our house," the older woman addresses Theodora with affection and esteem, yet without surrendering an ounce of the natural authority which she holds in her posture, her eyes, the secret empires of her body. "We'd always thought you would, and of course we hoped."

"I was always willing to do the work required." Theodora's back is screaming, and the skin on the backs of her legs is still red hot, but she is calm, basking in the blissful afterglow of her ordeal. "I knew what I wanted from the very beginning."

"You never know with the young," says the woman, "and you were so young when you started."

"Now you're fully initiated into our line," asserts the man, leaning forward a little and gripping the handle of his cane. "This will give you access to places which are not easy to attain to otherwise. You'll see."

"There are a small handful of others," says the woman. "Naturally we can't give you their names. Ours is a solitary line."

"You've told me a little bit about your contacts," says Theodora.

"The German man, yes, Mister Weber." The man relaxes back into his chair. "He worked with another woman about whom we know very little."

"We knew her as Alostreal." The woman casts her eyes toward her partner. "In the days before we came into contact with them there were the Theosophy groups, the coven, and our own work. Nothing we had found at that time had provided us with quite what we'd been searching for."

The man sips his scotch. Just over his left shoulder, from the place in which Theodora is sitting on the couch, can be seen a framed art piece resting on a high shelf above the red lacquer table. The piece depicts an image of a woman, skillfully drawn in black ink. She is naked but for a veil which conceals the lower half of her face. Inscribed upon the veil is the planetary symbol of Saturn. In one hand, the left, she holds a whip, in the other a sword, both pointing downward. The tip of the sword rests on the ground before the capital letter 'N', which seems to be inscribed into the earth.

The woman continues, "You've worked harder than anybody that we've seen so far. The work was necessary in order to purify your outer nature. That aspect of your character is now attached to something higher, and a different kind of work lies before you. After tonight your elemental soul will no longer be bound up with the body, rather it will have a house of its own in the astral light. That is its second house. If you continue with the work, you'll find that there's a third."

"And a fourth?"

"If there's a fourth," says the man, "then I have yet to catch sight of it. That would be beyond the point where we can lead you. You'll have to do that on your own, if such a thing is possible."

The man and the two women relax in silence for a spell. There's no sense of urgency, nor any need to fill the stillness which stands between them with idle chatter. After a time, the man takes his leave. The two women remain, never rising from their places on the couch.

"You'll have to find another if you want to perpetuate the line," says the woman.

"I'll want to."

"Of course you will. You'll add your own embellishments and flourishes, as have we. You'll find your own way of doing things. The line grows stronger as each person brings something of their own back to the work. Of course, if you were to choose not to pass the current on, your work would still feed back into the stream from which it came."

"And the source of the stream?"

"Lost," says the woman, a hint of severity in her voice. "As it should be, I suppose. It's partly a synthesis of other streams. Much of the instruction and the ritual can be traced back to earlier traditions. There are other aspects which I've not seen elsewhere, even after decades of study and research. Mysteries of every sort are preserved through the rituals and documents of countless initiatory orders, public and private. But there are other ways. There are a thousand traditions which course their way through history, very few of them spoken of openly. Each maintains its own particular Mystery, just as every stream consists of a water all its own. In some places the streams cross. Through centuries of admixture, new traditions arise, and the true Gnosis is clothed in new forms."

Theodora's wrists are chaffed from the ropes. She sits up and stretches, not without some pain.

"You'll have some lovely scars to carry with you once you've healed up," observes the older woman. "The secrets of our line have been impressed into your body. That alone will bear testament to what has taken place this evening. Of course you understand why our methods must remain secret. It keeps the line strong."

Theodora cannot help but grin a little. She shares a certain intimacy, if at a distance, with the older woman. Whatever may have taken place between them, they've entered into a wilderness frequented by few and have established a habitation of their own within it.

The conversation dwindles, giving way to sleepiness. Theodora takes her leave and makes her way through winding corridors back to her petite abode, perched over the ever-flowing waters of the night.

✳

Sebastian,

I've been away from the river for a spell. I've been travelling. I met a woman, whose face I could not see, in some dilapidated manor near the center of the earth. The crumbling façade of her time-worn veil serves to conceal something which mercy forbids us all from confronting face to face. Hers is a destructive wisdom which mutilates the soul and kills the heart. She reveals a side of nature which we are not otherwise allowed to see. It is vast and timeless, and has no regard for the particularities of the soul. Its enormous silence absorbs even the sun, leaving me with little but starlight by which to write this report.

In point of fact, I'm just now emerging from a most dismal bout of fever. I must have caught something from the damp, chill air down by the river's edge. I've spent an inordinate amount of time this last week sleeping or lying listlessly about. Delirium overtook me for a day and a night. At one point I became convinced that the river had overflown and was flooding my little town. I wondered how I might escape the rising waters as I drifted helplessly back to sleep. I was given to the most fabulous of dreams during this time, including one in which the inundation had submerged nearly the entire city, and the waters had come up to the level of the penthouse. A host of majestic birds had flown down from the sky and landed on the surface of the water and on the penthouse roof. They spoke to me and I understood them, though I don't remember a single word we said to one another.

I'm still not feeling quite myself. My body's wracked with minor aches; I scarcely leave my apartment but for brief walks beneath the stars at night. No sooner do I set out than exhaustion overtakes me and I'm disposed to return. I get stronger day by day. Soon I will be well again.

It's morning now. The sun emerges from its hiding place. Perhaps it will be a good day, after all. I think I'm starting to feel a little better.

(Continued after a two-day break.)

Much better now. I'm feeling myself again.

The solstice is almost upon us. There's a tradition that states that the sun is at the highest point in the inner world precisely when it's at its lowest point in the visible sky. It follows, then, that midnight on the winter solstice is the holiest time of the year. I can feel it approaching. The sun at midnight and the sun at noon touch hands through the veil for little more than an instant, but in that brief span of time they negotiate a contract. We are legally bound to this contract, as is everything upon the earth and under the earth. We are wise to keep within the bounds of this law. It is our own. The human animal is unique in its ability to deviate from its terms and conditions, though we bring about our own ruin when we do so.

The rain has followed the snow. It pours down from heaven and soaks the city to its very bones and sinews, washing the streets and gutters, pelting shop windows and arched roofs (the tiles of my rooftop have become so slick that I must take care to avoid slipping down onto the unforgiving stones below, baptizing them with my spilt blood).

I like to read the *Wake* by my open window as the rain comes down. The splash and patter of the rain, in its endless variety, occasionally falls into step with the rhythm of the text, while at other times the difference between them is so slight as to create a curious syncopation in which a third pattern arises, different from the meter of the rain or of the words, having virtues and vices all its own, and in which may be contained everything which is forbidden us to know. The Mysteries contained within the text are unfathomable, though I feel as if I've begun to find my footing in the topography of its vast abysses.

From spacious rooms with vast and vaulted ceilings
in palaces of sapphire,
River Station South,

Theodora

                                        ✳

                                  River Report #31
                                  December 27

Dear Sebastian,

Winter has settled into River Station South. The town is all the more beautiful for its advances. The solstice passed without occasion. I maintained an all-night vigil, which is not unusual for me these days (I sleep better once the sun's come up). My vigils have become increasingly relaxed as I grow older. I used to fast on the holy days. This time I simply read some passages from Blake and Shelley aloud and passed the time in contemplation of the year to follow. When morning came I set out on the town to share a glass of brandy with a friend who runs a bookshop in the northern quarter. We sat in silence among the shelves before she opened up her shop and enjoyed the spectacle of bodies moving to and fro in the bustle of the commencement of another day of work.

I stood upon the roof of my apartment late yesterday evening and invoked the Queen of the Tarshishim beneath the waxing moon. She is the Intelligence of the Intelligences of Luna and the Ruler with the Spirits of the Dawn: Malkah be-Tarshishim A'ad be-Ruach Sakharim. I called Her for counsel and guidance and was not disappointed, though I nearly froze in my thin black robe which billowed uncomfortably in the wind.

After the opening prayers and supplications had been delivered, and I had properly purified and consecrated the circle, fumigated the space, and anointed my body with oil of jasmine; after invoking the God of the Moon by the Holy Names of the Ineffable; after tracing the sigil of the spirit over a square of nine by nine with a drooping willow branch held in my left hand; after calling Her forth by name until my voice grew hoarse and my limbs were stiff from the bitter chill; after all of my effort and my toil, She took form before me, radiant in Her glory. She appeared to my inner vision clad in a gorgeous, flowing pale white robe woven from a moving mass of 28 lesser spirits. The writhing shades, one for each of the lunar mansions, appeared and disappeared in the shimmering folds of the luminous gown. Their voices rose to augment Her own as She spoke. She bestowed upon me secret knowledge of no uncertain virtue. We shared a sacrament of such refinement that nothing could defile it. We came to live a little in a house in the invisible, and there I died a little too. I'm not the same as I was before.

Here's another interesting thing: She told me that I could find the names of all of the lunar spirits written in a book which is hidden in a place which has no entrance. I cannot help but think that the hidden place referred to might somehow be found within the *Wake*. The fictions we partake of, as with the fictions we create, bear consequences for each of us that lie beyond the understanding and control even of their authors. If you meet me in Howth Castle and Environs, under cover of a starless night, I may reveal to you my inmost secrets or sock you in the eye. If I choose the latter, you will not complain. After all, what better way to prove you've been there?

The streets and rooftops of my town are covered with a paper-thin veil of snow. There's promise of more to come before sunrise. I wander aimlessly, leaving the first set of footprints in the frost. Moonlight bathes the fallen snow like the condensed breath of an intoxicated god. There's a certain levity in the air; I feel uplifted by the quiet joy which accompanies the coldest season of the year. Very few people leave the warmth of their houses at night to venture out into the freezing maze of streets and courtyards. I have the whole town to myself. I find solace on my solitary walk. There is a freedom which is granted only to those of us who are capable of living in two worlds at once.

There is little more to say. The poplars stand to attention in a line along the river, ready to defend it to their death if need be, not bothered in the least by the snow which adds its weight to their branches. A couple of crows conduct a mystery play in the slush outside my window. One of them slides down an icy sloped roof while the other waits below, squawking and flapping its wings. I watch in wonder as I sip my morning coffee. Their secrets remain opaque to me. The snow is beginning to melt in the rising sun. Later in the afternoon, when the snow has turned to muddy water, I'll go out walking along the river.

So, here we are. Another river report comes to a close. Nothing particularly cataclysmic has taken place around my domicile here on River Station South. The river flows by on a steady course, never deviating from its chosen route. My letters make their way to you in the beaks of pelicans (or so I like to imagine), and your silence or your absence speaks so loudly that I can scarcely hear anything at all for the cacophony. We are complicit, you and I, in acts of treason against the empire of the rational. Let us ever so remain.

In true service,
from a house with neither doors nor windows,
River Station South,

Theodora

Permutations of the Citadel

I

THE hands of the French provincial clock which hung above the reception area were arranged at some ungodly angle. The hour of the wolf had long since given way to the enveloping silence of the nameless hours. Algernon stood before a map of the hotel which hung in a modest frame of dark polished wood on one side of the grand staircase. Martin, sitting at the front desk, observed his friend's reflection in the large wall mirror on the other end of the lobby.

"I've been thinking," said Algernon, gazing intently at the map.

Martin raised an eyebrow.

"This map could do with an update. I think we might apply some creative editing; maybe add a room or two, remove a staircase, plant some extra doors where they ought not to be."

"I think that's a splendid idea," said Martin.

Not a doubt existed in Martin's mind that Algernon could pull off a perfect likeness of the map. Algernon had a way with imitation. He had trained himself to reproduce every conceivable style of handwriting and signature, no matter how idiosyncratic.

"It will be a trivial matter to remove the frame and glass," Algernon observed, studying the construction of the map. "Once we've come up with a suitable arrangement, I can draw it up. Nobody will notice what we've done for years."

Martin rose from the front desk and joined his friend. He regarded the contents of the frame with interest for perhaps the first time. As far as he could tell, no major changes had been made to the layout of the hotel since the map had been drafted. Quaint as it was, it was accurate at least. He placed a finger to his lips. "Diabolical," he said at last. "I like it. We can start planning the new layout in a bit. I've got Miss Pataki to attend to first."

"I can't say I envy you," Algernon lifted the map from its place upon the wall and turned it over to examine the back.

"Miss Pataki is somewhat of an acquired taste."

"I wouldn't claim to know," Algernon looked up from his study of the frame. "I've not yet set eyes on her, but from what you've told me I expect she's not to be trusted. I know the type. I can tell from your descriptions of her. She has an agenda, that one. I'd watch myself if I were you."

"Caution," said Martin, "is not my strong point. I don't count it as a virtue, in any case. Would you mind taking the front desk while I'm away?"

"Not in the least," said Algernon. "I could use the money."

It was a common practice between the two of them. Martin, who was officially employed at the hotel, would leave his post to satiate his wanderlust, while Algernon, who did not work for the hotel but knew how to perform

36

every detail of Martin's duties, would sit in for him. Money changed hands, typically about the same amount which Martin would have earned during the time that Algernon covered for him. The arrangement worked to mutual advantage. Their monetary requirements were few, and the job paid a reasonable wage.

Truth be told, Algernon was not wanting for money. He came from wealth, and every possible resource had been put at his disposal. He'd spent the greater part of the previous decade trying his damnedest to distance himself from his privileged upbringing. Letters from his family were answered sparsely, with a curt formality, demonstrating just enough effort to avoid suspicion. His trust fund stood untouched. He wished to live as the bohemians do; that is, to lead a minimal lifestyle without suffering any of the adversity which comes with real poverty.

Martin, on the other hand, had lived the life which Algernon only adopted as a pretense. He had lost both of his parents while he was very young as a result of the war. He grew up with an aunt, unmarried, who had barely managed to provide for him the basic needs of a growing boy. He watched helplessly, throughout his teenage years, as his aunt slowly succumbed to the ravages of dementia. He'd been living on his own since he was out of school. He was quite used to living in impoverished conditions. He had learned, from an early age, to nourish himself almost exclusively on the pleasure of his own company. He shared with Algernon the often unappreciated virtue of Solitude.

The quiet desolation of the hotel was, for the most part, left blissfully unbroken during Martin's shift. The occasional late-night check-in required a constant presence at the front desk. The guests rarely stirred after midnight or before dawn. This time of year was the easiest, the hotel register was sparse during the winter months. Most of the guests were travelling on business or cheating on their wives and didn't stay for more than a night or two.

Martin perambulated aimlessly through the expansive lobby, not quite ready to resign himself to Miss Pataki's embraces. The incandescence of the chandeliers conspired with the glow of the shaded lights that were mounted along the walls to suffuse the space in a soft golden luster, a luminous ambiance which gently highlighted the understated patterns of the carpet, the leather armchairs with their golden studs, the marble pillars which flanked the base of the main staircase.

A minute cache of literary treasures lay hidden in a recess on the inner side of the front desk. Algernon had made a habit of steeping himself in their eloquence and wisdom while he worked the lobby. Gustave Flaubert, Jan Potocki, William Beckford; these were his latest obsessions. He liked to sample them more or less at random, reading a selection of passages from one book before switching to the next.

Martin preferred to simply lose himself in the rich décor of the hotel, tracing the sumptuous patterns of the wallpaper with his eyes, or running his hands along the rich diversity of textures which presented themselves for his perusal. He had always felt that he might find, hidden among the rich details of the physical world, the means by which to pass beyond the veil of appearance and into something altogether different. The cathedral of the senses, he was certain, concealed a hidden chancel.

Leaving the solitary opulence of the lobby in Algernon's capable hands, Martin headed up the stairway to explore, for perhaps the thousandth time, the upper floors of the hotel.

＊

"In those days, I used a planchette," said Miss Pataki, "a beautiful piece of redwood, inset with a disc of amethyst. It was so easy. I merely focused on the inner eye and relinquished control of my left hand. I wore a blindfold, purely for effect." A trail of smoke wound toward the ceiling in slow spirals from the end of Miss Pataki's cigarette. She was easily twice Martin's age, perhaps more. She had about her every ounce of the magnificence of her years. She sat upright in the dark red leather armchair opposite the bed. Her lithe body admirably occupied an elegant silk dress of violet and mauve with silver buttons. The buttons which ran down the back of the dress had already been unfastened.

"With practice, I was able to do away with the planchette," she continued, gently tapping the end of the cigarette with one finger. A sliver of ash slowly drifted toward an octagonal ashtray of red and gold which stood beside the chair, touching down at last upon a decorative image of the head of Medusa at the center of the tray. "The voices of the spirits of the dead arose as if from a luminous haze just beyond the reach of the senses. It was simply a matter of tuning in to them. I was told that I had natural abilities."

She placed the cigarette in her mouth and began to unfasten the buttons on her sleeves. Martin lay reclined against the headboard at the far end of the bed, every inch a young man of taciturnity and reserve.

"Was it dangerous?"

"Probably," she said, taking the cigarette from her mouth. "I never completely surrendered control. I remained present, watching, like a passenger in the back seat of a car. I remembered everything the spirits said, even after the sessions. I wrote it all down in a series of journals. I still have them." She pulled her arms out of the sleeves and let the upper half of the dress fall away. "Most of them."

"You must have presented quite the spectacle," said Martin, hands behind his head, "with your blindfold and planchette."

"A hidden fire burned within me." Miss Pataki removed her stockings, one leg after the other. "I used it to generate fascination. It was child's play, really."

Martin remained silent. He was quite certain that, had ever a fire burned within his breast, it had long since been extinguished. "Why séances in particular?"

"It was somewhat of a forbidden thrill," she said. "Women of my social standing were not expected to participate in such nefarious activities. Society did not approve, and that suited me just fine." She considered for a moment. "No, I was drawn to it. It was a beginning, a way into something I'd been seeking for a long time. Of course it led to other things."

"What kinds of things?"

"Stranger things than I'd ever have imagined in those days." She rose from the chair and let the dress fall to the floor. "I'll tell you, but not now."

＊

Within a week, the map had been duly copied and replaced. Algernon had managed to find a perfect match for the paper in a specialist shop at which he was a fairly regular customer. His considerable drafting skill and access to the proper equipment allowed him to produce a near perfect duplicate.

The updated version featured several abnormalities which were unlikely to be noticed either by the guests or the hotel management. All of the rooms on one side of the sixth floor had been slightly shortened and a new room had been added in the space that remained. No door gave entrance to this room. Passage could be gained only by a staircase leading up from the floor below. The lower half of the staircase was omitted from the layout.

A second kitchen was added, identical to the first. It was placed behind the dining room, next to its sibling. Both rooms were simply labelled 'kitchen'. The first two floors had to be elongated on the map to account for the extra space.

The back wall of the lounge was altered slightly, so as to make room for an extra courtyard on the ground floor. This was simply labeled 'Palimpsest West'. From all appearances, the courtyard could be accessed through the garden court.

Further alterations were effected: a stairway rising to nowhere was added to an extra storage room, unnumbered, which had been made to fit into an unused area of the basement; the freight elevator was moved a considerable distance to the south; two further rooms were added to the second and fifth floors, one of them was labelled

'The Archivist', the other 'The Anchorite'. The finished piece was in every way a work of art. Algernon had taken great care to give to it the ring of authenticity.

Nearly a fortnight had passed before Martin again found himself in the company of Miss Pataki. They stood out on the balcony of room 413, illuminated by a single candle which shone from a dresser inside of the room. They sipped champagne beneath the stars and luxuriated in the pleasure of each other's company.

Earlier that evening she had given him a pendant containing a hand-carved piece of cinnabar suspended on a thin silver chain. "A talisman," she said, "imported from China." The smoky red mineral set within the pendant featured a fine octagonal border, inside of which was carved an intricate floral design. A vertical bar ran from the upper edge of the octagon to the lower, twisting and turning at several points along the way at right angles.

Leaning against the rail of the tiny balcony, Miss Pataki pointed out a single star which shone like white fire in the northern sky. "That one is the lowest star in the sky at this particular latitude that never sinks below the horizon," she said "The stars which never set have something of the eternal about them. They remain perpetually awake. Their number increases as you proceed further north."

"Tell me more about the séances," said Martin, clutching the pendant in one hand before him.

Miss Pataki turned again to face him. The faint glow of the heavens graced the contours of her countenance. "They were amusing enough while they lasted," she said. "My events were frequented by every type of occultist, and by artists, musicians, writers. I held them in the upper section of the duplex I was renting at the time. They occurred every second Sunday. The guests would arrive at dusk. After the séance was over, we would have an informal salon."

"Would that it were possible," said Martin, putting the pendant back into the breast pocket of his shirt. "I would love to have attended them."

"Would you?" Miss Pataki regarded him with incredulous eyes over the rim of the champagne glass. "You strike me as the quiet type; reserved, kept to yourself, so different from the boorish socialites my parties tended to attract."

"I observe, I listen, I absorb," Martin placed his hands together. "I become invisible in social situations, but I walk away from them with intimate knowledge of the personalities involved. Anyway, do continue."

"There really isn't much more to say. I quickly became bored with them. The séances never did deliver what I'd been looking for. I met a man through the salons, an initiate of the Mysteries of the Rose and Cross, or so he claimed. We began a series of experiments, just he and I. We did quite a bit of work together."

"Go on," said Martin, intrigued.

"We learned to part the veil between wakefulness and sleep. We worked primarily with mirrors. Did you know that a mirror, if properly employed, can be used to reveal hidden doorways between this world and the next?"

"You are positively an obscurantist," said Martin dismissively. "I assume you employed language no less cryptic when you hosted your séances?"

"You don't attract the cream of London's intellectual crop by speaking in unfanciful terms, darling." She held the champagne glass in the fingertips of both hands. "Mirrors offer a unique means of perception. Reflected light reveals a world of color, while direct light is invisible to us. Just as we perceive the natural world through our senses, we perceive the world beyond through an instrument which is subject to certain . . . limitations."

"The soul," said Martin.

"A French scholar of esoteric Islam, who used to make occasional appearances at my soirees, once referred to it as 'the sensorium of the imaginative faculties'." One hand gently rested on the balcony rail behind her, fingers stroking the iron as if to enflame the very metal. "I'll tell you more," she said, stepping away from the rail and back through the balcony door.

Martin followed, hands in pockets. Miss Pataki lowered herself with an aristocratic grace into the armchair opposite the window. She placed the champagne glass on the table beside her while Martin made himself comfortable on the bed.

"We were shown things, my partner and myself, which we were never meant to see," she continued, half bathed in shadow. "We furnished a temple. Two of them, in fact. One of them resided in this world, the second one was fashioned on the other side of the mirror. Each of them was a reflection of the other, do you see?"

"I'm not so sure that I do," said Martin.

She ran her finger provocatively around the rim of the glass. "They were constructed according to particular specifications," she said. "We took great pains to ensure that the angles of reflection were correct. Work of this type is very difficult. All it takes is a tiny miscalculation to distort the image."

"But you managed it."

"We managed it," she said.

❉

Martin sat at one of several tables strategically arranged around the dining hall. The elegance of that part of the hotel had always appealed to him, with its eggshell-yellow pilasters and dignified cream wallpaper, the round gold-framed mirror above the fireplace, the diffuse radiance shed from the elaborate chandeliers above. He sat opposite a row of windows which peered out into the desolate night, idly turning the pages of an antiquated atlas found some weeks ago in one of the storage rooms.

He became aware of a distinct trace of unease as he perused the old maps, noting the differences between the national borders which were shown in the atlas and those of the modern world. He looked up from the book and glanced about the room. There was something peculiar about the two arched doorways at either end of the far side of the dining hall. Both doorways led to the kitchen, allowing the staff to pass in one side and out the other. He'd never noticed it before, but the space seemed rather wide given what lay behind it. He'd been through the kitchen many times before, and had thoroughly inspected all of the cupboards, drawers, cabinets, and refrigerated spaces found therein; it seemed like such a small space compared to the wide stretch of wall which separated it from the dining room. The notion so unsettled him that he felt compelled to get up and have a look.

He entered through the left-side doorway. It opened onto a little vestibule and from there into the kitchen proper. It was just as he'd remembered it—short and compact, an efficiently organized cookery of no great size. He continued on, passing through the doorway on the other side and back into the dining room. He felt certain that the wall on the dining room side was much longer than the same wall on the kitchen side. How could he have never noticed this before?

After a minute's thought, it occurred to him to try and pace out both sides of the wall. With carefully measured steps, he traversed the space from arch to arch along the dining room. He counted 16 paces. He repeated the procedure in the kitchen, liberally beginning inside of the vestibule itself so as to avoid underestimating the distance. He had scarcely taken 9 paces before he found himself passing through the doorway on the other side. He was perplexed.

Back in the lobby, he studied the map which he and Algernon had altered, paying specific attention to the two kitchens. Might they have altered the map, he wondered, in response to something which had already been observed just beneath the surface of consciousness? Martin stared furiously at the floor plan, as if, by sheer intensity of effort, he could somehow come to terms with the spatial anomaly.

"An older couple came by late last night," said Algernon from behind the desk. "I'd forgotten to tell you. They were admiring our work. I think they might have caught on to our little scheme. I'd meandered over to the mirror, pretending to inspect the frame for dust, and I saw them pointing to the citadel."

"Pointing to the what?"

"The citadel is my name for the unlabeled room on the top floor which doesn't have an entrance," said Algernon. "I think it's quite appropriate."

"The citadel," repeated Martin. "But what is it meant to defend? The hotel?"

Algernon considered the question for a moment. "It defends itself," he said.

Martin briefly considered returning to the dining hall. He thought better of it. He placed a finger upon the second kitchen on the map as if to fix it into place. "I suppose I can take over the front desk again," he said.

"Good by me," said Algernon, closing his book and rising from the chair. "It's best that I leave early tonight and try to get some sleep. My father's in town tomorrow. I've got to take lunch with him. I can't get out of it."

"I suppose it's an unspeakable horror to be forced to share a meal with your family," Martin felt a pang of envy, not having been afforded the luxury of choosing the conditions of his own exile.

"It is an unspeakable horror, in point of fact," retorted Algernon. "Aunts, uncles, brothers in law, half-cousins— not a single one among them care in the slightest what I might want or what type of person I might be. I'm expected to become one of them, to join their ranks and prove my worth to the world.

"Over lunch, my father will ask me, for the thousandth time, precisely what I plan to make of my life. He'll insist upon an answer as he always does, and will not cease to pester and belittle me until I squeak out some insignificant lie to make him happy. As it happens, I don't want to make anything of my life. I want merely to pursue my obsessions. I don't live in my father's world, nor do I adhere to its laws. I would live and die in anonymity, a tiny voice arising momentarily within the multitude. That's all I want."

Martin was somewhat taken aback. In the years of their friendship, he had never once heard Algernon speak so emphatically about anything. "Well, Algernon, you can certainly count on my support."

"I appreciate the sentiment," said Algernon, "but there's nothing you can do, nor anybody else. I may be written entirely out of my family's history, but I'll have my way. The world will scarcely know that I existed."

*

Later in the week, Martin lay in the lazy embrace of Miss Pataki on the bed of room 413, nestled like an oyster in its shell. He was not entirely certain that there wasn't a pearl between them, if well hidden. There are intimate secrets which are shared between two people that cannot be divulged in any tongue. Miss Pataki smelled of musk and amber, mingled with a curious scent which Martin could not quite place. Even her natural fragrance suggested traces of the inaccessible, the forbidden. She had a curious ability to remain perfectly opaque while appearing to bare the inmost chambers of the chapel of her soul. Martin felt an affinity with this trait. He seldom felt comfortable around people who revealed too much of themselves.

"Do you ever get lost wandering around the hotel?" asked Miss Pataki as she rose to fetch a cigarette from the open pack upon the dresser.

"The place isn't very big," replied Martin, sitting up and propping himself against a pillow. "I don't see how I could get lost."

Miss Pataki lit the cigarette, dropped the match into the tray, and returned to the bed. "You might employ particular strategies," she said. "There are ways of losing yourself within familiar places."

They finished the cigarette without another word. The sweet smell of the smoke mingled with the scent of Miss

Pataki's skin to produce a rare and exotic spice at once enlivening and soporific. Something of her character, or so it seemed to Martin, had made its home in every aspect of the room. She always chose to stay in room 413, though he had never once seen her check in or out of the hotel. She was in the habit of leaving a note for him with the front desk on the nights that they were to meet. The notes were kept short and discreet. The room itself was not a luxury suite, yet it was not without its charms. It was unique. It was a corner room. Windows looked out to the south and west. To one side of the dresser stood the glass door which opened onto the balcony. Milky white curtains hung to either side of each of the windows. The taint of cigarette smoke was just faintly visible near the tops of the walls and on the ceiling.

A little while later, as Martin was about to leave, Miss Pataki stopped him. Smoke poured in luxurious tendrils from her mouth and nostrils. "The pendant I gave you," she said, "why don't you see if you can find a use for it?"

＊

Algernon sat in a chair before the vast mirror in the lobby, thoroughly immersed in the barbarous revelations of *Salammbô*. Martin sat at the front desk studying the pendant that Miss Pataki had given him. Suddenly he stood, placing the pendant in his breast pocket. "Mind watching the front desk for a bit?" he asked.

"Certainly," replied Algernon without taking his eyes from the page.

Martin, given to a peculiar notion, took himself up several flights of stairs and down a hallway to the door of the now vacant room 413. Facing away from the door, he removed the pendant from his shirt pocket, running his fingers over the exotic red mineral with its intricate design. He assumed, for the sake of experiment, that the vertical bar which ran from the upper section of the octagon to the lower could be read as a sort of map, indicating a series of directions to be taken from a chosen starting point. The first bend in the bar announced a right turn immediately outside of the door. He surrendered his fate to the obscure dictates of the cinnabar, passing beneath the soft glow of the overhead lamps.

He followed the pendant through several junctions, his route taking him all the way down to the first floor and thence along a short route through the basement. The path came to an end before a series of storage rooms which had once been used as sleeping quarters for the kitchen staff.

Martin glanced at the row of closed doors which lined the corridor. He was certain that the hallway harbored only five rooms, yet six doors lay before him. The door at the very end of the hall was unnumbered. He was intimately familiar with the layout of the hotel. Something was clearly not right. The extra door would seem to correspond exactly with one of the unnumbered rooms which he and Algernon had added to the hotel map.

Martin stood before the errant door. He placed a tentative hand upon the knob. If it was locked, he mused, he ought to be able to fetch the key from upstairs, though he wasn't entirely certain which key to look for. He turned the knob and pulled. The door opened without difficulty. Immediately behind it lay an ascending staircase, just as the map indicated that there should be. Leaving the door open on its hinges behind him, Martin climbed the stairs with a certain amount of trepidation.

He emerged into a tiny, empty room. The far wall was entirely occupied by a tinted window through which could be seen a view of the hotel lobby. Martin realized with a start that he was standing in a space concealed behind the large mirror opposite the front desk. A moment's glance, however, revealed a view quite different from that of the lobby which he had stepped away from only moments before. The entire space was bathed in shadow, illuminated only by dim shafts of light from the chandeliers at the top of the stairway. Rolling waves of thick white smoke poured forth in a voluptuous tide from somewhere off to the left. Smoky tendrils crawled along the high ceiling as if with tainted fingers, encroaching onto the territory of the front desk and extending toward the stairs. The smoke was illuminated by the flickering of an open flame, which was also out of view.

All of the hotel furniture was gone. The floor, normally carpeted, was covered with smooth white marble in a horrible state of disrepair. Many of the tiles were cracked or otherwise disfigured. The wood paneling on the walls was deeply stained with filth. Gaping holes appeared in several places. Large sections of the back wall had been destroyed completely, revealing a framework of decayed beams through which glimpses into other rooms, similarly ruined, were exposed. The pillars on either side of the staircase were lamentably chipped and gouged, their surfaces blackened with grease and soot. The dark wood of the stairs was thoroughly rotted through. The whole space looked as if it had been left unattended for decades on end.

What's more, the bodies of several small reptiles, stout and black with yellow blotches, darted to and fro amidst the wreckage. A handful of the beasts, salamanders from the look of them, could be seen crawling along the surface of the mirror, their bellies sliding across the dark glass as they made their way from one place to another. A tiny horde of them furtively emerged from a wide breach in the wall behind the rotted wooden shell of the front desk. They scampered off in every direction, disappearing amidst the rubble and the filth.

An exquisite work of smooth white stone protruded from the wall just above the front desk, the single item in the spectacle of ruin which had not been subject to decrepitude and waste. The body of a woman carved from ivory was displayed from the navel to the crown. Her imposing presence presided over the space as if she were its secret patron saint. A face of benevolence and wonder was crowned with crescent moons. Her iridescent hands, luminous and delicate, supported a pearly sphere within their fingertips before her naked breasts. The radiance of the image provided a stark contrast to the wreckage and decay, like an icon of holy grace erected in the bowels of perdition.

No sooner had Martin taken in the audacious display than the solitude of the lobby was transgressed. A fleet-footed woman with pallid skin and a head of dark curls stepped gingerly forth from the far left, one foot placed before the other as if engaged in some sort of ritual dance. Her lithe limbs glistened in the flickering light of the flames behind her. She wore only a time-ravaged gown, once perhaps elaborate but now reduced to tatters, ancient as the night itself.

Swiftly, swiftly did she advance, one bare foot placed before the other, darting toward the staircase of rotting wood. She paused before the threshold marked by the two pillars, strenuously arching her body as if to entice some unholy god. She raised one hand high above her head. From its clutching fingers dangled, by its silver chain, the talismanic pendant of red cinnabar. The other hand produced a long, silver whistle which she placed to her lips as if to call forth the legions of the damned. Dark eyes peered out through the curls, eager with anticipation. Her cheeks puffed out dramatically and the whole space was bathed in a horrible peal of disharmony.

Three short bursts she played upon the infernal instrument, each one more jarring than the last. As if in response to the dissonant signal, a rustling flock of finches rushed around the corner from above the grand staircase. They poured forth in multitudes, black and brown and yellow and white, issuing forth at tremendous speed; a cataclysm of fluttering wings which cast a dubious orchestra of shadows upon the floor beneath them. They advanced in a seemingly endless stream. One thousand tiny birds were followed by one thousand more. They filled the upper hall, they congested the canopy of the staircase, they flocked en masse into the ravaged amphitheater on the other side of the darkened glass, they swarmed in and out of holes in the walls and ceiling, they threatened to consume even the dark-robed woman who had called them. Only the ivory statue remained untouched, too holy to be disgraced by the ravages of the flock.

Thick smoke continued to pour forth from out of view. Before a moment had passed, the lobby was obscured and all that could be seen were the salamanders on the window and a horde of shifting shadows cast by the flutter of innumerable birdwings. The glass of the mirror creaked and groaned, unable to bear the heat from the other side. Martin felt a tingling numbness in his fingers. His breath stopped short in his chest just as the mirror shattered. By the time the first shards of glass hit the floor, he'd already surrendered to the sweet oblivion of unconsciousness.

II

There exist certain classes of phenomena, Martin strongly felt, which are best kept to oneself. He mentioned nothing of what he'd seen behind the mirror to Algernon. He deplored the notion of keeping secrets from his friend, but then he hadn't quite accepted the reality of the experience. In any case he didn't think that he could find the words to describe it. Nor did he deem it appropriate to discuss the matter with Miss Pataki. He kept the memory of the scene veiled in silence, as if in a vessel which had been hermetically sealed.

He had woken in the basement corridor, lying on the bare concrete before the doors to the storage rooms. He scrambled to his feet, looked frantically up and down the hall, and was relieved to count only five doors along the northern wall. He checked the right breast pocket of his shirt, then his trouser pockets; the pendant was gone. When he returned to the lobby, Algernon was still sitting in the exact same chair as when he'd left him, thoroughly absorbed in his book. The two scarcely spoke a word for the remainder of the night.

Later in the week, Algernon requested a small favor. In accommodation to his request, Martin retrieved the numbered plates from several of the guest-room doors, taking care not to break the seal of the paint as he pulled them from the surface after removing the tiny screws. Particular room numbers had been specified. It was clear that Algernon had a coherent design in mind.

Martin lounged on a covered divan in the lobby while his friend painted bright red figures on the backs of the thin brass plates from his place behind the front desk. "There's a method to my madness," declared Algernon. "I've formulated a secret code using the Kaballah of the Hebrews." He painted seven plates in total, utilizing six letters of the Hebrew alphabet: Samech, Pe, Reysh (this letter appeared twice), Shin, Ayin, Yud. "The letters each have a numerical value," he went on. "They're meant to combine with the numbers on the plates according to a particular scheme. There's one for each floor, with the repeated letter in the basement."

"Nobody will ever find them all," Martin reclined lazily, gazing up at nothing. A slight gray smudge which appeared in the very center of the high ceiling gave him a start. It looked almost as if the spot had been burned, just a little, by a fire from below.

"All the more glory be to the God of the ancients," proclaimed Algernon. "True Mystery abides ever concealed from the profane." He proceeded to write several cryptic messages on long strips of paper, the text derived from anecdotes found in Beckford's tale of the wretched Caliph. These he rolled up tightly and gave to Martin, with instructions to place them behind the numbered plates of several further doors. "Every part of this project comes together into a perfectly realized whole," he said. "If any one person were to unveil my design, they would find themselves confronted with the thumbprint of a grand conspiracy between angel and architecture."

Martin carried out the tasks he'd been allotted, happy to contribute to a project so deliciously obscure. A flash of motion caught his eye just as he was refastening the metal plate to the door of room 412. Peering down the hall, he spotted a dark streak which seemed out of place. It quickly disappeared around the corner of the hallway. Martin softly crept down the length of carpet and around the corner. Clinging to the lower section of the wall several doors distant stood a black and yellow salamander. It scrutinized him with cautious curiosity before making its way into one of the heating vents. Martin refused to allow this to disturb him. Having replaced the last of the numbered plates, he headed to the lounge for a quiet glass of wine before his rendezvous with Miss Pataki.

✳

"A temple is a place of contact between the visible and the invisible," said Miss Pataki through a violet haze of smoke. "A proper temple must adhere to certain geometric principles." She was dressed in an elegant silk kimono of dark turquoise which extended all the way to her ankles. Moonlight streamed in through the open balcony door and collected in pools of luminescence in the folds of the fabric. She sat at a little table by the window while Martin reclined on the unmade bed.

"I always thought of a temple as a place of worship," he observed.

"There is an element of devotion, if not worship." Miss Pataki crushed the cigarette on the octagonal tray which stood behind her and immediately lit another. With the same match, she lit the candle which stood between them. The flame illuminated the flat, black label of a bottle of Bordeaux on the windowsill.

"The ultimate aim of devotion," continued Miss Pataki, passing the cigarette to Martin, "lies in the annihilation of the self in the beloved."

"Why on earth would you want that?" Martin took the cigarette and placed it between his lips. The subtle flavor of Miss Pataki's lipstick, recently re-applied, lingered on the filter.

"In the temple, the second temple, I found precisely what it was that I'd been seeking in the séances," she said. "Our work together, my partner's and mine, reached a sort of apotheosis in that space. I was made a recipient of keys which have been passed down from teacher to student for as long as anybody can remember."

"The pendant you gave me." Martin had not entirely formulated the question he wished to ask.

"Do you like it?"

"Very much," he said. "Thank you."

"You might treat it as a compass," she said, the surge and flicker of the candlelight caressing the shadows of her face. "It is befitting for a young man of your type and disposition to maintain proper orientation."

Later they sat together on the balcony sharing a glass of wine, Miss Pataki leaning back against the curvature of the iron railing while Martin lay against her, her arms gently enfolding him. She held the wine glass before him and tilted it back. Martin could just make out the reflection of the Pole Star in the surface of the dark, red liquid.

"I used to scry the stars this way," she said. "I'd catch the reflection of the star I wanted in a glass of wine, like this one, and I'd use it as a doorway. Sometimes it took some time. I was patient in those days. The reflection would eventually give way to a cloudy mist, and I'd receive a vision. When the vision had ended, I'd drink the wine as if it were a consecrated host."

"What did you see?" asked Martin, calling briefly to mind his experience on the other side of the mirror in the lobby.

"The northern stars revealed the most," answered Miss Pataki. "The far north was once considered to be a place of mystery, an inaccessible region which was forbidden to us. Travel in the more extreme latitudes was, in the distant past, associated with the attainment of a type of immortality."

The glass exchanged hands. Martin gave the contents a gentle swirl, causing the wine to rotate counter-clockwise around the chamber. He'd always wondered whether the direction in which the wine was swirled made any difference. He took a sip, allowing the subtle flavors of the intoxicating nectar to fill the cavern of his mouth: tobacco, leather, a hint of cherry.

"Did you know," asked Miss Pataki, "that in the middle ages the north side of a church was said to belong to the devil?"

"I did not know that," said Martin, nearly able to relax in Miss Pataki's tender embrace.

"A lot of old churches in Sussex still have a door in the northern wall," she said. "The devil's door, they used to call it. The north door is bricked up in some churches, in others it's so small that it's of no practical use. There are, however, churches to be found from place to place which may be entered through that door, though it's said that if you enter through the devil's door, you may find yourself in the devil's church."

"And what might you find in the devil's church?" Martin turned around to face his mistress.

"The devil's architect," she said without a trace of irony.

Long afterward, just as the first rays of the pre-dawn sun had begun to taint the serenity of night, they feasted on fresh fruit and fine chocolate, washed down with more wine. Martin wanted to ask about the pendant that she'd given him, and about the mirrors and the temples and several other things besides, but something held him back. He sensed a certain reticence on her part to explain too much. He yearned to know more, but didn't wish to overstep his bounds. Accordingly, he kept his tongue concealed in the sanctuary of his mouth.

Martin kept an eye out for irregularities within the hotel grounds over the following weeks. He had almost come to regard the building as a sort of cathedral, a place of sanctity by which the seeker after mystery might be led, as if through a labyrinth, into communion with an intelligence greater than his own. His regular trysts with Miss Pataki, the countless hours spent wandering the halls, the games which he and Algernon indulged in—these seemed to take on an attitude of prayer, as if they comprised a sequence of incantations designed to facilitate the parting of a veil.

Occasionally he would catch the odd glimpse of a retreating salamander as he wandered through the corridors. The place would seem to be infested with them. He expected that the management, or at the very least the cleaning staff which worked during the days and early evenings, could not have failed to notice their presence, so he said nothing about the reptiles in his nightly reports.

A close inspection of the mirror in the lobby revealed nothing of particular interest. He'd hoped, perhaps, that he might discover a hinge or some other method of separating the glass from its mounting on the wall, but nothing of the sort presented itself. A careful exploration of the layout of the first floor demonstrated, without much room for doubt, that there could not possibly be space for a hidden room between the wall on which the mirror was mounted and the lounge area on the other side of the wall.

"Be wary of mirrors," said Algernon, looking up from the tangled convolutions of Potocki's *Manuscript Found in Saragossa*. He sat reclined upon the platform between the upper and lower sections of the main stairway. "They can't be trusted."

"I should rather think not," answered Martin. "Aunt Agatha became increasingly uncomfortable with mirrors as she was overtaken by dementia. I don't think she entirely believed that it was her own reflection which was looking back at her. It got so bad that all the mirrors had to be taken out of the house. She had begun to break them in fits of rage."

"I'm not entirely certain that she was mistaken," said Algernon, looking every bit the figure of a devilish young man under the light of the chandeliers. "Reflected images can be treacherous. Perhaps your aunt simply saw through the deception."

Martin was less than enthused with Algernon's line of reasoning. That notwithstanding, he regarded the reflection of the lobby in the surface of the mirror with vague suspicion. He pressed his face up against the glass and cupped his hands around his eyes, hoping to catch a glimpse of something on the other side. Nothing but darkness stared back at him.

The nights which followed passed without incident or revelation. Miss Pataki was as alluring and enigmatic as ever. Algernon maintained his usual reserve, expressing himself exclusively though his disdain for the established world and by way of incomprehensible works of frivolity. Martin remained slightly on edge. The loss of the pendant had made him particularly anxious. He felt as if he'd been irresponsible with the gift from Miss Pataki, though he couldn't imagine how the indiscretion might have been avoided.

Late one night, as Martin studied one of the portraits above the grand fireplace in the ballroom, it occurred to him that he might return to the dining hall to try and locate the extra kitchen which had been added to the map. He hadn't set foot in that part of the hotel since his experience behind the mirror. He'd been somewhat apprehensive. He felt that these things must be approached with a certain restraint, a certain amount of respect for the unfathomable. He sensed that it was time, though he couldn't say for what exactly.

He didn't have a specific plan in mind. He only had the vaguest idea of what it was that he was trying to accomplish. It should be possible, he thought, to slip into the gap within the space of the hotel between the contours of the original map and that of the altered map, and thus to find a means of ingress to that long sought after place which was at once completely foreign and intimately familiar to him. In any case, he'd done it once, he ought to be able to do it again. He retrieved a length of rope from one of the storage rooms and made his way to the opulent hall.

Martin sat at one of the tables near the kitchen entrance and knotted the rope at approximately every third foot. Entering the kitchen through the vestibule, he laid one end of the rope down by the entrance. He somehow felt, without quite understanding why, that the extra space would stay put so long as he could positively account for it. From one side of the kitchen to the other, he counted six knots. Continuing on around the corner, he laid down thirteen further knots along the dining hall wall. Entering the vestibule again, he laid the rope around the corner, and was astonished to find that the other end of the rope did not appear on the floor before him. With a shudder up the spine, he realized that he was standing in the second kitchen.

Martin let the rope fall to the white, hexagonal tiles at his feet. As far as he could tell, the second kitchen looked exactly like the first. A salamander scuttled along a row of cooking pots suspended from hooks above a counter. It darted up the side of an overhead cabinet and disappeared among the exposed ventilation shafts above. Cautiously, as if he might somehow shatter the delicate boundary between one world and the next, he made his way to the doorway on the other side. He passed through the archway and into a place utterly different from what he'd expected.

The pungent smell of aromatic smoke assailed Martin's nostrils, momentarily disorienting him. Square metallic tiles of yellow and gold lay beneath his feet. They were not quite fixed into place, and the clatter of their slight displacement echoed throughout the cavernous hall as he walked over them. Decorative walls of red stone carved with elaborate designs stood largely chipped and ruined around the perimeter of the hall. Dilapidated pillars, worn with age, supported grand arches between them, dividing the hall into several chambers arranged around a central alcove. Large cracks gaped in several places on the stone floor, many of them half-covered with tiles. Rolling clouds of incense, along with the occasional salamander, emerged from the fissures. The black and yellow reptiles, too many of them to count, crawled over the metallic tiles on the floor, along the cracked and elaborate stonework, up and down pillars, and beneath stone arches. Finches soared in tiny swarms above, occasionally alighting on crumbling blocks of masonry. Tall yellow candles flickered inside of wrought iron lamps which hung from the high ceiling.

Two flaming torches which stood in the main alcove directly before Martin cast a bewildering array of shadows among the labyrinthine complex of marble and stone. Between the torches stood a throne of sorts, a low tripod of silver upon which sat a woman robed in rich scarlet. She perched imperious on her divinatory seat, back rigid, chin elevated. Upon her closed eyelids had been carefully painted a pair of open eyes in bright red. They gazed directly ahead, penetrating and indifferent, contemplating an invisible horizon. A cloth of dark crimson was draped over her head, falling in silken folds upon her bare shoulders.

The shadows flickered across her face like the beating of crow's wings in a windstorm.

Set into the stone floor before the sibylline figure could be seen a silver plaque in which a title had been engraved: "The House of Somnambulism".

Immediately before the tripod stood a low table upon which sat an open book. A quill and inkhorn lay next to the book, of which the visible pages were blank. As Martin approached the throne, the woman leaned forward as if guided by wires. With an elegance of motion befitting a vehicle of hidden wisdom she picked up the pen and scrawled, in letters facing Martin so that he might read them without effort, "Ask."

Martin took a moment to consider his words. The question was drawn forth from deep within him as if evoked by the oracle. "How can I reach the citadel?" he asked.

Without a moment's pause, the hand of the oracle wrote out a response while her shoulders and torso remained rigid. Martin leaned in a little toward the book, so as to make out the neatly penned message.

"Is the citadel open to you?" she had written. "You bear the mark of your impetuosity. In your innocence, you have violated the holy place and inadvertently absconded with the veil of Tanit. The current of your breath has been tainted by the winds of Moloch. The citadel lies before you, unseen, and yet you cannot find the door."

Martin looked upon the face of the Sybil. Dispassionate, painted eyes gazed through him. He stood at last before the very heart of Mystery and he was determined to apprehend the wisdom thereof. "How might I gain entrance?" he asked the oracle.

She leaned forward in an elegant arc, writing drifting toward the empty half of the page. Her hand scribbled furiously as her body remained motionless. Before a moment's time had passed, the ink had dried on the completed message: "You must traverse the boundaries of an invisible cube. You've blindly traced its vertices, yet one side is still unknown to you. By permutation, you may find the hidden intersections. You've inherited the gift of blasphemy, use it. Here we invoke essences sacred and profane in unacceptable combinations in the hope of gaining insight into the topology of the ineffable."

The body of the Sybil remained immobile above the book while the smoke of the incense traced calligraphic epiphanies around the legs of the tripod. Martin pondered briefly the enigmatic nature of the answers thus far given. "Might the archivist be of aid to me?" he inquired.

The oracle scrawled out a swift response. "You may divine messages from the archivist in the patterns on the carpet, the complex layout of the tiles upon the floor, or the paths of light and shadow reflected in adjacent mirrors. Let a blueprint of the architecture of the invisible be your holy book. Pray to a God obscure enough, and you may be given access to places forbidden even to the priests."

"And the anchorite?" Martin continued.

"Your one desire should be to satiate him," wrote the oracle, with a steady hand. "He is eternal in his solitude. He alone has completed the sequence. It remains only for you to recover it."

Martin hesitated, unable to formulate another question. The Sybil, having uprighted herself, again leaned forward, sphinx-like, as if to pose a challenge. "Your inquiry has been sufficiently answered," she wrote.

Martin stood before her, unsure of how to respond. "Indeed," he said at last.

One hand turned the page of the book while the other, gripping the quill, glided into place above the virgin sheet. It seemed that the oracle intended to convey a final message. Suddenly, her body stiffened beneath the scarlet veil. She shuddered and jerked, trembled and convulsed, the quill gripped rigidly in one hand. Her slender frame contorted as emanations from ineffable tongues coursed through the temple of her body. After a few tense moments, the turbulent seizure subsided. Her robed torso raised itself upright as if lighter than air, her chin was elevated, and she once again assumed the dignity of her sacerdotal office. Again she leaned toward the open book, quill in hand, and began to transcribe. When she had finished, Martin leaned in close to read what she had written.

"You are far from understanding," he read. "Let yourself sink beneath the surface of the waters. We are of the drowned, the fallen and forgotten. Do you fear oblivion? How we long for absolution in death! Carathis, the mother of abominations, abides in a place as yet unknown to us. We cannot comprehend her emanations. We've sought for her in vain, yet have found nothing but the mask of our own wretchedness. It is little consolation to us that the Caliph has fallen. We have yet to find the space left by his absence. Now, leave this place. I have nothing more to offer you."

Martin looked once more upon the face of the oracle. She sat motionless upon the tripod. Without a word, he rose, turned, and was confronted with the choice of which door to take back to the kitchen. It took him scarcely a moment to make his decision. He headed for the vestibule opposite the doorway by which he had entered. The modest entryway had been replaced with an elaborate stone arch. Would this route take him back to the kitchen, he wondered? And, if so, which of the two? Determined to see his ordeal through to the end, Martin continued through the tunnel of stone.

He was not, however, in the slightest bit prepared for what lay before him. He emerged from the oracular temple onto a dilapidated wooden platform, stained with grime and soot. He stood beneath a vast canopy of blackness. He couldn't quite discern whether or not he was still indoors. No stars appeared overhead, nor could he see any trace of a ceiling through the dense clouds of smoke which roiled and gathered in baleful formations above.

Far beneath him lay a vast and terrible expanse. A seemingly endless landscape stretched out to a horizon obscured by cloud and smoke. The parched earth below was studded with burning garrisons and crumbling towers, great pylons crisscrossing the dark soil, mineshafts and tunnel entrances leading deep beneath the scarred and rocky surface, and monstrosities of brick and steel half concealed in shadow and smoke, all interspersed with uniformed bodies moving frantically about in an ecstasy of labor.

Flaming torches partially illuminated white statues which protruded at obtuse angles from the tortured ground. The statues took the form of vast human figures in a variety of enigmatic poses. The plaster was cracked and broken in several places, covered with moss and grime, permeated with decay. They appeared as wayward gods arising from a subterranean sleep.

Perplexing monuments had been erected or discovered in the open labyrinth of night, illuminated at their bases and extending upward into the darkness, their peaks unseen. Men and women wearing uniforms of military design were organized in groups both large and small. They carted soil and masonry from place to place, fired bricks and cut blocks of ashlar, planted torches in the earth, and shouted orders as they proceeded among the ruins in complex formations.

In the far distance could be seen a tremendous edifice, an enigma of fire and iron. It towered far above the other statues and structures which stood arrayed amid the darkness and the smoke. Its arms were raised up toward the sky as if to bring down the wrath of the starry heavens. The head upon its massive shoulders, thrown back and twisted in a monstrous howl, resembled that of a tremendous ox. Imposing horns protruded from above the ears, penetrating the thick sheaves of darkness and fog which gathered about it. Apertures gaped from its hulking breast, gleaming with the light of a thousand gems plundered from the bowels of the earth. Fat black cauldrons were arranged before the statue in a semi-circle, rising columns of impenetrable smoke pouring from their mouths and into the darkness above. Such an abomination could only be the likeness of Moloch, the God of the Phoenicians, the reconciliation between deity and beast.

Martin simply gazed in wonder at the vast expanse before him, much of which was obscured by smoke which poured forth from the mouths of cavernous pits leading deep into the earth.

III

Algernon sat at the front desk, awaiting Martin's return. As Martin descended the grand staircase, bathed in the diffuse glow of the rich chandeliers above, Algernon barely looked up from the project in which he had immersed himself.

"I can take the front desk now," said Martin as he shuffled along in a semi-conscious daze.

"If you don't mind," Algernon looked up from his work, "I'd like to make use of the surface for a while longer. You don't have to pay me."

Martin didn't mind. As Algernon hadn't volunteered the information, he thought it best not to ask what he was up to.

"Something's not quite right with the hotel," Algernon announced, head still buried in his task.

"I've noticed as much," said Martin, noncommittally, taking a seat near the bottom of the stairs.

Algernon looked up. "You've seen it then?"

"Oh yes."

"They'll blame us for anything that's happened, you know. Well, you anyway."

"I would think that would be the least of our problems," said Martin.

"Speak for yourself. I'd hate to lose this job." Algernon went back to what he'd been doing.

Martin let his body sink into the soft leather of the chair, head rolled back and eyes closed. Thus he sat for the better part of an hour as his tattered nerves slowly unwound. At last, he took a deep breath and rose from the chair.

He glanced over to the front desk, taking a sudden interest in his friend's project. The hotel's complete reserve of 'Do not disturb' cards sat to one side of the desk. Several further cards sat before Algernon, some of which were blank, while others bore messages which were painted in the same style as those of the original stack. Martin approached the desk so as to better see what Algernon had done. Three of the seven cards before him had been completed. Algernon was just beginning to sketch out a message for the fourth. 'Do not fathom' read the first, followed by 'Come not by water', and 'Creep hither and break upon uncharted altitudes'.

"They've been getting more elaborate as I go," said Algernon, looking up briefly. "Eventually, somebody's bound to notice and will probably do away with the lot, but who knows how many will have been in use by that time?"

Despite the unsettling experience from which he'd so recently emerged, Martin was amused. "Algernon, you're an absolute genius," he said.

"I think so."

＊

Martin sat at one of the low, black tables in the lounge enjoying a glass of Merlot. He often spent a little time in the darkly painted enclave before wandering off into the other areas of the hotel. Large, black-framed mirrors flanked the entrance. A grand piano occupied the center of the room. Martin poured a tiny bit of wine onto a saucer which he'd retrieved from the dining hall. He felt that an offering to the spirit of the place was in order. He hoped to entice whatever it was that presided over the threshold between one side of the hotel and its reverse to reveal to him, once again, the hidden means by which to infiltrate the inaccessible regions.

Black wooden bookshelves rose from the floor to the

glorious ceiling along one wall of the lounge. Among the tasteful spines bearing the titles and authors of several classic works was displayed a set of encyclopedias, twenty-nine volumes in decorative black and red with two further volumes comprising a dictionary and thesaurus. Martin rose from where he was sitting, walked over to the book-shelf, removed volume seventeen from the set, and took it back over to the table. He cracked open the heavy volume and paged through its contents until he came to the entry on 'Polaris (Star)'. The entry occupied the top half of the left-hand column of the page. Martin produced a fountain pen from the breast pocket of his shirt, removed the cap, and carefully wrote a message in the outside margin.

> Francesca: Meet me at precisely 3:15 a.m. in Palimpsest West. I will bring 360 mg opium, a compass, and the dog whistle (you know the one). We will act swiftly. We will not hesitate. We will do what must be done.
>
> In fires of passion which threaten to con-
> sume the very soul,
> and rightful trepidation,
>
> The Archivist.

Martin left the book open, sipping his wine while he waited for the ink to dry. A minute passed, maybe more. He closed the book, rose from the table, and replaced the volume in the vacant space upon the shelf. Draining the last remnants of his wine, he placed the empty glass up-side down before one of the mirrors. He liked to leave the odd item lying about to irritate the morning staff. Having nothing more to do there, he made his way to the upper floors of the hotel.

✳

Miss Pataki had fallen into a pensive silence. She had ceased to regale Martin with stories concerning her past exploits. It was as if she had revealed too much, and had reverted to an introverted attitude of restraint. She sat upon the bed and smoked her customary cigarette. Bare arms emerged like those of an ancient statue from her dress of shining gold. Contemplative and slightly distant, she seemed to Martin to have veiled herself in the stillness of the night.

"I don't suppose you can tell me anything about the citadel?" he asked, scarcely hoping for a response.

The look on her face might have passed for annoyance had it not been so elegantly framed. "Citadel," she said with measured coolness, "comes from the Latin root *civis*, meaning 'citizen'. The Greek word is 'acropolis', which translates roughly to the highest point within the city. I don't know that I have anything more to say on the matter."

Martin, for the moment disposed to pointed questions, pressed on. "Where did you get the pendant which you gave to me?"

Miss Pataki took a long pull from the cigarette. She turned toward the window, the smoke pouring out in extravagant curls from her voluptuous mouth. A moment later, she crushed what remained of the cigarette upon the tray and turned back to Martin. "Are you going to make love to me, or not?"

"Yes, Miss Pataki."

✳

Finches, speckled black and brown, occasionally flitted about the upper reaches of the ballroom in pairs or groups of three. It would appear that a nest was hidden somewhere above the panels set into the high ceiling. Martin took note of this as he pulled open the tall balcony doors and stepped out into the pallid moonlight.

He leaned against the marble rail of the balcony and aspired to the sanctuary of night, to mysteries unspoken, to the primal gnosis sought in ancient, unwritten, and forbidden rites. He'd tasted of the fruits behind the veil in recent months, yet still he hungered. He wished only to penetrate further, to pursue the invisible beloved to the very heart of the temple.

The past several weeks had been spent in a fruitless search for a way back into the hidden reaches of the hotel. He'd studied every inch of the map, followed every lead he could think of within the hotel grounds, probed dead-end hallways and freight elevators, traced perplexing patterns through the corridors and stairwells; he'd carefully searched the perimeter of the building in hopes of finding some inconsistency or otherwise stumbling across a means of ingress. Nothing had turned up. It was almost as if the doors which he so desperately wished to find could be located only by accident.

Along the way, he'd noticed several irregularities, to be sure. Salamanders stalked the hallways in surprising numbers. Finches flew about along the stairwells and through the open spaces of the hotel. He'd found the remnants of several of Algernon's past projects and a few of his own which he'd forgotten. Meanwhile, Palimpsest West was closed to him, he could find no trace of archivist or anchorite, and the citadel lay ever beyond his reach. Even Miss Pataki had fallen silent, choosing to reveal to him nothing more than the time-honored rites of the pleasures of the flesh. At last he'd given up, content to wait for the mystery to approach him on its own terms.

With a deep, resounding sigh, Martin turned around to face the building. He arched his back just slightly over the lip of the marble and gazed up at the edifice of stone which, though it had revealed something of its secret depths, still concealed from him its inner sanctum. He closed his eyes, head leaned back, and gave himself up to the encroaching blackness. A single word jumped to his lips, softly whispered: "Moloch." He faintly recalled a distant pain, a pang of forgotten suffering which he dared not name. He opened up his eyes. The black iron balcony of room 413 could be seen jutting out from its place near the southwest corner, and beyond it, the balconies of the upper floors.

Something caught Martin's eye. He counted, as best he could through blurred vision, the sixth-floor balconies. His heart jumped just slightly. There seemed to be an extra one among them. And what's more, a light appeared to be shining from the room beyond. It could only be the citadel!

Martin wasted not a minute in gaining access to the roof. He'd been atop the building many times before. It afforded a fantastic view of the city. It was accessible via a tiny hatch which was set into the ceiling next to one of the stairwells. The key was found at the very bottom of the rack behind the front desk. It was unmarked, but a simple process of elimination was all it took to deduce its purpose.

Martin made his way to the southern edge of the building. He approached the waist-high concrete lip, leaned over in anticipation, and was pleased to find that the anomalous balcony, bathed in pale yellow light, lay more or less directly below him.

Cautiously, he put one leg over the threshold, judging the distance to the surface below. The drop from concrete lip to iron rail was about twice his own height. The balcony was not large, there was barely enough room to support two people at close quarters. Martin was terrified to consider the possibility of falling from such a distance. He put the other leg over, sitting on the rim. The balcony lay immediately below him. He stilled himself, turned around and grabbed the smooth edge of the rim with both hands, let his body go slack so that his feet hung below him, and dropped. Almost instantly, the soles of his shoes smacked the iron slats of the balcony floor, causing the carriage to shudder ever so slightly. He sat there for a moment, leaning against the curved iron railing, and stared into the space which he'd been so ardently seeking.

The room, narrow and petite, was bereft of furnishings or décor of any kind. There was nothing but a single chandelier, standard for the hotel, hanging from the center of the ceiling. The light cast by the decorative bulbs illuminated the upper reaches of a staircase leading down below. After what may have been a minute, perhaps more, Martin rose and tried the balcony door. It swung open, unlocked.

Stepping with caution, as if trespassing in a holy place, Martin took himself to the top of the stairs. The stairway descended only a short distance before it was submerged in a liquid fire of dazzling whiteness. He stood above the heart of the citadel, gazing down in eager anticipation upon the waters of the lunar baptism, the fires of absolution, the untainted substance of pure, reflective mind, the naked visage of Tanit unveiled.

The Salamander Angel

Finally, when we have understood the secret of the Black Stone, we will understand that the secret of the Temple is the secret of man, and that he who has grasped it has the keys of the Temple in his possession: on him has been bestowed the potestas clavium.

—Henry Corbin
The Configuration of the Temple of the Ka'bah

Breaking and Entering

MARITA kneels by the river flowing swiftly swiftly through the heart of the night. As she rests upon the soft earth she prays fervently to her star. That star, that secret gnosis, appears in all of its splendor before her, pouring forth lines of numinous force on which she is quite carried away. Upward she travels, as swiftly as the winding river, upward into the soft light of the heavens. There she passes through the heavenly palaces and into the secret houses, even into the dark heart of the forbidden places. At last she is returned to the earth and to her body as before, yet now she bears within her breast a hidden secret flame. Is it the Word unspoken, issued forth in silence from the tongues of angels? Yea, the volatile has been fixed! The secret knowledge is with her now, and she knows exactly what to do with it. Off she goes into the night. Thus Marita.

Peter, meanwhile, meanders through the city's nocturnal streets and byways as if exploring the cherished body of a lover. He seeks the hidden places, lost empires of neglected beauty, the voice of the beloved cast within the very stones. The dark poetic soul of the city beckons to him from all quarters, drawing him down unlit alleyways and into desolate expanses. The transgressive star Capella shines brightly overhead, sacred to vagabonds and wanderers. Gently guided by its emanations, Peter drifts aimlessly from square to thoroughfare.

It would be unthinkable for a young man to court the urban muse without the proper attire. Peter wears the uniform of a man who would remain invisible. He adorns himself in unremarkable greys and blacks, well-worn yet tasteful. Long black hair lends a smattering of character to an otherwise unfortunate face. He is the very soul of wanderlust insatiable.

The wind picks up and the leaves become increasingly sparse at his feet as tree-lined avenue gives way to squalid service road. Along deserted loading docks, among dilapidated factory buildings, around the crumbling remains of an old school long since closed, Peter pushes on into the unfamiliar, letting himself lose his way as he reaches toward the heart of the night. A bare light bulb warms a lost, foreboding doorway set within a brick enclosure; darkened windows gaze listless and despondent at the cloudless sky; discarded mail carts lie supine all in a row amidst a stack of rusty iron beams awash in tawny light; the lifeblood of the city flows through the disregarded spaces revealing buried veins and forgotten arteries among the refuge and the waste.

At length, Peter comes upon a crumbling brick edifice which sufficiently fires the lusts of his imagination as to warrant a more thorough probing. An ornamental frame harbors two sets of double doors, both secured by heavy chains which are wrapped around the handles. Thin, arched windows reach toward a crumbling peaked roof. It is an old, abandoned church, judging by the Calvary cross cut into the brickwork. With little forethought, Peter resolves to find a way inside.

He circles around the perimeter of the building, looking for a possible entrance. An empty window frame sits not too high above the ground on one side of the church toward the back. Peter jumps and grabs hold of a rough brick ledge which forms the base of a lower window, pulls himself up, and is just able to reach the next ledge higher which allows him entrance into the holy place. He manages to scramble through with little effort.

Dust clouds leap in extravagant arcs as Peter's feet strike the floor. Light cast down from a row of windows near the ceiling faintly illuminates the dilapidated interior. On the far side of the church stand the double doors comprising the proper entrance. Alcoves sink back into the walls on either side, holding nothing but a pocketful of dust and ashes. Pews line the floors, some knocked over and others askew. The wood is shot through with mold and rot. Niches in the walls near the entrance are adorned with raised pedestals, their bases reaching just a little higher than Peter's head. Fairly elaborate statues stand upon the pedestals, two on either side of the church. They depict somber-looking men draped in flowing robes. One casts his eyes heavenward, another turns to look behind. A third stares straight ahead with great intentness, while the last of them wears a rather perplexed expression, as if confronted with an apparition which he cannot fully comprehend. The statues are in disrepair, showing signs of age and neglect. Chunks of broken masonry lie at their feet; broken fingers, bits of wing, the cracked flourish of a robe.

Within the chancel on the other side of the church, harbored in the rounded apse and flanked on either side by a row of empty candle-holders, stands a monument to piety rendered in stone. It is an angelic figure, female, larger than the others and far more elaborate. She is a creature of grace and beauty. Wings stretch out behind her back. Her palms are cupped before her as if to catch the excrements of stars. Her face is stern and devout with but a trace of holy dread. Beneath her waiting hands stands an altar of rotting wood, its decaying exterior highlighted by dim shafts of moonlight that shine in from a circular window above..

Peter stands in awe for just a moment. Blessed is the star which has led him to this place! He bows down low and kisses with his lips the scum-encrusted concrete. Rising, he walks about the church, letting his fingertips run over the chipped brick and stone, inhaling deeply of the musty odor of decay and the resonance of age-old frankincense and prayer. It is as fitting a house of God as Peter ever saw.

Returning to the center of the church, he faces the altar and sits, eyes closed, carefully regulating his breathing. When Peter was still in his early teenage years, he found in the attic of some boarded-up house a stack of old books which, decades past, had been distributed by a local Theosophical society. These became his manuals of instruction. He began to practice the techniques found therein and quickly attained to a mastery of the art of astral projection. It was as if the surface of the world were but the superficial skin of a much larger edifice, and he had learned to pierce that skin and penetrate into the depths beyond. The shifting architecture of the visionary light became a secret country for him. Over the years he's managed to refine his technique, having found further esoteric keys by which the hidden waters may be navigated.

Peter fashions, in his mind's eye, an image of his own likeness standing a few feet before him. A quick projection from the invisible eye in his brow sends his point of view from the grosser body to the subtle. In his finely woven vehicle he rises into a church of visionary light. The spirit of the place has long since etched its contours into the soft and malleable substance of the soul of the world. It is subject to the phases of the sun and moon, the emanations of the stars and planets, the inpouring and outpouring of the breath of God, and the invisible influence of the uncharted hours of the night.

The Salamander Angel

There is a knock on the door. A moment later a squat, rectangular panel slides open revealing the decorous eyes of a young woman.

"What's the secret password?"

"Huffenpuffen."

"Nope."

"Blatherflap."

"No sir."

"Ramplatherer?"

The door is opened slowly, revealing Unit in all of her splendor. "Welcome to the region of insufferable squalor."

Simon strides in, heads directly to an elaborate little bar decorated in wrought iron and red velvet, and pours himself a cognac. His glass is ceremoniously elevated just above his head and swirled twice clockwise to no discernable purpose before its contents are swiftly emptied. "I consecrate me with hootch," says he, tossing the glass over one shoulder where it lands gently on the carpet.

"Charming. Are you just going to sit there and drink my liquor, or are you planning to help me set this thing up?"

"I must apologize. I am a cad. Unit, my darling, you look ravishing!"

"And you look like some kind of armchair theologian," she says, "but I suppose you'll do. Help me push the furniture back so we can get started before the sun comes up."

Simon does as he's told. He does in fact look remarkably studious, dressed in silk vest, undershirt, jacket and pressed slacks. He takes great pains to look the part of the occultist, cultivating at once a mannered image and a measure of theatricality. He keeps his hair at an unfashionable length, and yet he manages to look every inch a gentleman.

Unit, on the other hand, is endowed with a natural flamboyance which no amount of affected coarseness can obscure. Rarely does she apply more than the scantest trace of make-up. Her wardrobe is intentionally kept quite modest. She has her hair cut plain. And yet, as if cursed by a host of houris, she is never less than radiant. Her face reveals the tenets of a lost art. The mysteries of her bodily proportions astound the most cunning of the Kabbalists. Her appearance is not beautiful as much as it is arcane. Simon shares with her an intimacy which few others are allowed, if only because, despite his flippancy, he really is quite devoted to the art.

The pair push Unit's turquoise leather couch back up against one of the two large bay windows which span one wall of the tiny apartment. They stand the little ornate coffee table upright against the bookshelves. The carpet is rolled up and shoved beneath the couch. There is just enough room in the space that remains for two people to move about without feeling cramped or crowded.

Unit's apartment, small though it is, is an island of exoticism in the heart of decrepitude. Bookshelves of black polished wood line one wall, filled with rare volumes bound in leather alongside various busts and other curios. The remaining walls, hand-painted in an intricate pattern of reds and yellows having an Arabic motif, are decorated with framed artwork too audacious and obscure to mention. The horned head of a petite gazelle, a true marvel of taxidermy, resides above a little doorway leading to the balcony. The whole is lit by a simple, yet elegant red chandelier.

The setting for a ceremony is prepared. Candles made from pure beeswax are set up in a circle, sacred names inscribed thereon. Plates are brought out from the kitchen containing little cakes, which are placed in the east. Prayer books are opened to particular pages and set out before the candles. A bottle of strong liquor is placed in the west. Simon drags an altar into the center of the arrangement and Unit proceeds to decorate it with bells and candles, a phial of oil, an incense burner and an elaborate sigil painted on a piece of parchment. A minor arsenal of wands, daggers, cups, and pantacles are placed to either side of the altar. Finally, the robes are brought out from the closet and laid across the couch.

The scene is set for an invocation of the Salamander Angel. Few more than a handful of passing references to this obscure divinity exist in the classical texts, save for one lengthy passage found in a surviving fragment attributed to a student of the Gnostic Valentinus. In this passage the angel is said to be nameless or having a name that cannot persist upon the tongue. The angel takes the form of a woman, or a blazing star, or that of a fiery salamander. The author of the passage had received the tidings of the blessed angel in a vision which culminated in gnostic awakening. The body of the angel was then revealed to the mystic, each part associated with a fragment of its secret name, all of which is specified in the text. The piece continues: "This I am permitted to reveal that I may share my revelation with the wise, for I have brought down Truth from her supernal dwelling, that those who may bear such wisdom may see her naked and come to know her beauty. Here is the source of every word, the origin of every voice, the utterance of all that is unutterable, and the mouth of silence. These are the echoes of the ineffable names that adorn the Divine Throne, the habitation of the great and terrible God, whom none may look upon and live."

Initially known only as Aletheia, or 'the unconcealed', the enigmatic figure was later worshipped as the Salamander Angel. She appears thus in the writings of the Sabians of Harran, and much later in a handful of grimoires attributed (falsely so) to several among the great minds of the ancient world. The Salamander Angel is referred to always as a bestower of hidden gnosis, a teacher of forgotten tongues, and an initiator into mysteries immeasurable. Giordano Bruno penned a lengthy poetic description of her virtues. A text attributed to John Dee arranges the names attributed to the parts of her body into a series of elaborate grids and tables. She appears even in modern times, celebrated by a local surrealist group which flourished briefly before the war. One of them created a sculpture of her likeness which to this day stands before the University Library.

Simon and Unit have stepped out onto the balcony to share a cigarette before the rite begins. An ornate iron railing prevents them from toppling down onto the street below. A small, square platform rises from the center of the railing at waist height. On top of the platform sits a wooden chessboard with several pieces missing. The remaining pieces are so arranged as to suggest that a game is in progress. The last glimmer of sunset has long since withdrawn its majestic radiance, abandoning the city to the fathomless waters of night.

The balcony affords a tantalizing view. Located between the industrial and university districts of the city, Unit's apartment occupies an ill-defined zone of overlapping neighborhoods. A river can be seen winding in the distance between several squat factory buildings and successive rows of dilapidated houses. Cafes, night clubs, boutiques and establishments of ill repute stud the urban landscape. They reside like wayward stars torn free from their orbits and condemned to cling to the surface of the earth. Pale orange light shines out from open windows, illuminating the shadows and exposing the interiors of countless kitchens, parlors, dining rooms and sleeping quarters.

"Algol's rising over the university." Unit indicates the spot with the lit end of the cigarette. "Her constellation is the head of Medusa, severed at the neck by the blade of Perseus. The influence of the star was considered a terrible blight by the ancients, but I've always felt an affinity with her. She will bring a benediction to our work."

"The demon star shining over the place of learning. I can't imagine what could possibly go wrong." Simon moves a white pawn from one square to the next.

"Philistines always demonize the things they can't understand," says Unit. "The gorgon's star is also said to be an incredible source of arcane wisdom. Soon she'll be directly above the very spot where the statue of our angel stands, in front of the library."

"A perfect conjunction for book burners and heretics," observes Simon.

"The star bestows a light that surpasses understanding," Unit continues, ignoring him. "What more exalted blessing could we possibly ask for? The Salamander Angel merits nothing less."

"I do suspect that you are taking elaborate pains to hurtle us headfirst into oblivion," says Simon. "I applaud your actions in that regard, to be sure, and you know that I'm loathe to advise caution in any case, but do you really think it's wise to so flagrantly court the ire of the heavens? Sometimes I wonder if you're overcompensating for something."

"We all march toward death, Simon. There's not a single thing of worth we stand to lose." Unit lifts a bishop between two slender fingers. "I wish to give myself entirely to the absolute. Wisdom is that which destroys, if for no other reason than that nothing can contain it. It doesn't know half-measures. You have to be willing to let yourself drown in order to attain to it. I aim for nothing less." Toying with the bishop for a moment, she places it arbitrarily back onto the board.

"You're like a captain on an expedition to the arctic wastes," Simon inserts a hand into his jacket pocket. "I can imagine you on the deck, looking fabulous in your uniform, yet I fear your crew would abandon ship before you left the harbor." Simon raises the cigarette before him, moving a knight with his free hand. "In any event," he says, "I will not abandon ship, my captain, though you lead me where no man may trespass."

"Men are always so afraid to break the rules." Unit grips the iron rail. "Heaven has no use for those who are afraid to sin. Our holy books tell us that there was a mutiny in Heaven once, a host of angels rebelled, brought the arts and sciences to the dwellers of the earth, and for this they were punished. Fallen angels, they call them. This is obviously a man's point of view. The true key to the Mysteries is excess. Effort must be sustained until a boundary has been crossed. It's not enough to fill your cup if you would storm the gates of Heaven. It must be made to overflow."

"Spoken like a woman on the verge of self-annihilation. In any case, we poor men can't possibly hope to compete with such blind ambition. On behalf of my gender," Simon bows at the waist, "I officially hand over the keys to the kingdom."

Unit gently kisses his bowed head. "You silly man. I already have them."

"I must admit," says Simon, rising once again, "your recklessness excites my grosser sensibilities. I believe it was Oscar Wilde who said that women were to be heard, not understood. You're like a sphinx on a drunken rampage through the sanctuary of gnosis, a mystery to God and man alike."

"Are you any less a mystery to yourself?" Unit moves a pawn two squares back.

Simon raises the cigarette to his lips and partakes deeply of the fruits thereof. "Alas," he concurs, letting the smoke pour from his mouth, "I must admit, I understand myself no better."

"The more you know, the less you understand." She takes the cigarette. "We can never truly know anything, Simon, least of all ourselves. There is a limit to understanding."

"I am a fool to trust you," Simon sighs, "but to do otherwise would be intolerably boring, and I would hate to think myself a sensible man. I would prefer to fancy myself a man of untamed passions. Let us cast our shackles to the wind!" He turns to face her. "Forget the ritual—make love to me at once!"

Unit appears to consider for a moment, casually picking up Simon's rook. "No." She tosses the rook over the rail of the balcony and onto the street below.

They finish their cigarette in the hushed embrace of night. It is customary for them do their work in the later hours while the city sleeps. Rising early is abhorrent to the natures of them both. Their professional lives accommodate their preferences. If you walk beneath the balcony of

Unit's apartment late at night, it is just possible to catch a brief glimpse of her hacking away at her laptop, her head and shoulders illuminated by the soft glow of a single lamp. You may even catch her standing on the balcony as the sun comes up, with nothing but a cigarette to keep her company. If the curtains are drawn, you can be sure she is engaged in arcane theurgic rites.

The night's work is soon to begin. The hour is nearly upon them. The technical aspects of the rite are gone over one last time. There are preliminary prayers and ablutions to perform, a circle must be established, the space must be properly consecrated and the ritualists anointed with oil. The cakes will be offered as bribes for the guardians of the astral gates. Liquor will be poured for the intoxication of the fiery serpents that keep watch over the threshold. Figures must be traced and holy names intoned, gestures given and circumambulations performed, all while making sure that the space remains properly fumigated with the sweet-smelling smoke of the incense.

"Henceforth we go into the mouth of the night," Simon proclaims with index finger raised, "that we may commune with the noetic fire of the midnight sun!"

"I promise I will smother you with kisses if you would shut up for just a minute." Unit is getting the last bits of wax out of a candle-holder so that a fresh taper may be inserted.

"Cursed be the angels of my intellect and wit! I simply cannot do as you ask. It's not in my nature. Besides," says Simon, "I am quite certain that you lie. I fear I'll need to resort to unfortunate extremes in order to collect the debt."

"I always pay my debts," murmurs Unit, "I just pay them on my own terms is all." The last of the wax removed, she steps inside to complete the furnishings, returning a moment later. "Now pass me the cigarette," she says, "that I may temper my contempt."

"Oh, you crush my heart with your cruel barbs!" Simon is truly taken aback.

"My disapproval is not directed at you, this time." Unit casts her eyes down toward a group of men in suits noisily making their way out of a popular night spot across the street.

"The upwardly mobile," she sighs. "They sit outside at the café and keep me up all morning with their dreadful power lunches and their conference calls."

"Well, it's only fair isn't it? The invisible influences that emanate from your apartment must haunt their dreams."

"They *enhance* their dreams . . ." Unit considers for a moment. "Oh, I probably do haunt them, don't I? The poor, miserable fellows. It can't be helped. They live in a different world than we, only we have to share the overlapping spaces." She takes one last drag, and hands what remains of the cigarette to Simon. "The men who play at managing affairs of great importance in the world are like frail sheets of rice paper. They have no destiny. They're blown aimlessly about by the dictates of the market. If they were to look within themselves and find any trace of a soul, they'd renounce it or lose it in some meaningless transaction. They are little more than facades. I hate them."

Simon lets her disdain stand unanswered. He isn't entirely certain that anything lies beneath the surface of his own facade. He stares out into the empty night. The vast menacing specter of the world does not respond to anything he says or does in any way. He's fashioned for himself a shelter from its cold indifference, erecting walls that even he can't breach. Yet Unit has managed to surmount them all without the slightest bit of effort. She has exposed the iniquities of his inmost soul, and seems to have accepted them. Simon clings to her for sheer terror. He regards her as somewhat of a force of nature, a living monument to mysteries that he will never fully comprehend.

The cigarette butt is flicked from the balcony into the cold embrace of starlight. "Let's get started."

The Lodestone

Somewhere in the heart of one of the more remote neighborhoods of the city lies a modest tenement building of little more than 50 units. Tiny windows set within a lush display of moss and crumbling brick reveal domestic scenes of unimaginable variety, a rich anthology of stories never told. Few of them are of any interest to us. We must limit our attention to a tiny selection of crucial elements if we are to derive anything of meaning from the unparalleled events which are unfolding in our midst.

An open widow set high within the brick facade gives way to a sparsely furnished apartment full of disarray and clutter. Bookshelves crammed with impossible objects line the walls. Here you will find star-globes, primitive counting machines, sextants, pendulums of every variety, tuning forks, canisters of dirt and sand, phials containing liquid mercury or any number of other substances, finely calibrated scales and other measuring devices along with countless books and notepads crammed with loose papers. Sitting at a work desk with not an inch of visible surface is a bespectacled man of anxious disposition who spends his nights engaged in tasks which are obscure to anybody with a shred of decency. Making use of compasses and protractors, dark minerals and oscilloscopes, geological maps and water table charts, Oliver works diligently into the night in pursuit of the unattainable. He seeks, in his labor of unrequited love, to chart the elusive topology of the soul of the Earth.

What is Oliver doing now? What dark designs have captured his obsessions? He is poring over ancient maps of the Temple of Jerusalem, diagrams of Mecca, depictions of Sabian star temples, and floorplans of the Tabernacle. Polygonal antechambers topped with domes of polished ivory seduce his imagination. Heavenly basilicas fraught with angels of judgment or mercy betray perverse geometries in no way reconcilable with the work of human hands. Messianic decrees forge contracts between the temporal and the eternal within the contours of the Holy City whose blueprints are spread out before him.

Scores of maps line one side of the work desk. They are filled with notes and sigils and crisscrossed lines. With the assistance of the pendulum, of radionic analysis and several geomantic charts, Oliver has mapped the meridians of Microprosopus upon the habitable regions of the world. The scope of his studies has narrowed over the years to the confines of the city in which he's lived all of his life. Again and again, as if pointing with the hand of fate, all lines have converged upon a modest church, long since abandoned, not far from his very building. Was it a site of worship in ancient times? A meeting place for secret assemblies? A safe house for fugitives and criminals? It has served in all of these capacities and more. It is a place of natural resonance, a place in which harmony persists between the sacred and the profane.

Between a set of cloth-bound books containing a preferred translation of The Zohar and several volumes from the works of Ibn 'Arabi sits an ornate wooden humidor topped with tempered glass. Oliver rises from his chair and takes his place before the box. He places his fingers on the mahogany finish, unseals the brass clasps with his thumbs, and lifts the lid. Inside is a rough, black-brown stone about the size of an acorn. The box and its contents are lifted from the shelf and taken back over to the writing desk.

Oliver sits. He removes the stone and weighs it in the palm of his hand. His fingers close around its rough, uneven surface. It exerts a slight pull disproportionate to its weight. Oliver's closed fist feels almost as if it were being tugged gently toward the stone's core. It doesn't feel quite like the pull of gravity or the attraction of a magnet. There is simply a subtle urge to let the object remain enclosed within his palm.

Oliver received the stone as a gift from a dying grandfather more than a decade ago. His grandfather had worked as a physicist, serving at the Academy of Sciences for most of his life. He made several notable breakthroughs in the study of radioactive isotopes and cosmic rays. After receiving a handful of awards he was sent off to Tomsk to work on a project about which he was not able to talk openly. One year later he returned for a brief respite, then was sent back for another two years. Each time he returned, he was sent back for a longer period than before, until many years had passed and relations with his wife and son had all but been abandoned. Oliver was seven by the time he'd met him, and although, or perhaps because, there was a pronounced sense of tension in the family surrounding this strange gentleman, they formed a natural sodality between them. They maintained a close alliance in the years that followed. The two would often stay up long into the night on family visits, remaining thoroughly engaged in conversation after everybody else had gone to bed.

Oliver visited his grandfather frequently toward the end of his life. He alone did this. Nobody else in the family found much time for an old man who seemed to be losing his mind. Ah, but what a mind to lose. Long rambling monologues through thick dark woods of scattered recollection would open out onto lucid vistas of visionary brilliance, only to plunge back into the depths of senseless anger or sentimental reverie. Oliver had infinite patience for the tirades and the tears. His love for the man was genuine. He would hold the old man's shaking hand until it was forcibly pulled away and balled into a fist, curses spat out against the child who had practically disowned him and the wife who shared her bed with one colleague after another. A minute or two of silence would pass and he would forget his troubled feelings, and the kind and gentle man who was Oliver's mentor would return.

He often spoke in caged terms about his work in Tomsk. It was no secret that it was in that frigid city that he had acquired the stone. Might it possibly have had some connection with the famed explosion in Tunguska? Vague indications that this might be the case were occasionally let slip. His grandfather was not forthcoming with details concerning the matter. A dogged taciturnity was maintained regarding the stone. Probing questions were answered with a change of subject. Oliver was able to ascertain only that the old man seemed a little bit afraid of the thing.

Oliver extends his fingers, gazing at the stone in the bowl of his palm. All outward appearances would indicate that the dark mineral is a magnetic lodestone. Exhaustive experimentation, however, has revealed properties differentiating it from other stones of its type. Chemical trace analysis has yielded vaguely perplexing results. It has been found to emit electromagnetic impulses not quite in line with what one would expect. Nor is its density quite consistent with its mass. Tests of a subtler nature have given rise to astounding implications. Oliver has submitted it to every type of divinatory inquiry, always with frightening results. It is a special thing, having a particular purpose. Oliver has reason to believe that it may be used as a sort of key.

The lodestone is placed in a small cloth bag and set upon the desk. Oliver walks over to one of the bookshelves lining the far wall and removes a periodic journal, one of several in a series. He places the journal on the desk next to the cloth bag. On the cover is an ink drawing of a figure with two faces, each looking in the opposite direction. Looking to the left is the face of a woman, stern and authoritative; to the right looks the face of a man in an attitude of reflection. Many arms extend from the body, some holding objects while others seem to grasp at nothing. The feet of the enigmatic icon have been replaced with hands, while the heart opens up into the mouth of a cave extending down and back beyond the confines of the body. The title 'Rebis' appears above, while beneath it is the following byline: 'We will submerse ourselves in the waters of night that the drowned may be resurrected.' In smaller print the reader is informed that this is the seventh edition of the journal, issued during the winter solstice of 1938.

The journal was issued with regularity on the solstices by an association of avant-garde poets based in the city. Its publication continued for a period spanning little over half a decade. The actions of the association were suppressed during the Soviet occupation, during which time most of its members scattered across Europe. In its early days it was run like a secret society of sorts, holding clandestine meetings and subjecting new members to initiatory ordeals. Their public manifesto made allusions to such conventions as the building of a new Jerusalem, the reestablishment of the temple at the center of the Earth, a secret tradition of heretics and prophets working in unison throughout history to perpetuate a gnosis of perversity and dissent. Among the most notable of the association's works was a tremendous statue of the Salamander Angel. This was sponsored by a wealthy patron and donated to the city 'in order to affect a transfiguration of destiny, that the lost Word of antiquity may be restored to us.' The statue miraculously escaped censure during the occupation, remaining in place through the following decades of Soviet rule.

Oliver flips through the pages of the journal until he finds a sought-after page displaying the poetic supplication of a celestial intelligence. With heavy heart, he rips the page from its bindings and places it next to the journal, which he then closes and replaces on the shelf.

A fresh sheet of writing paper is taken from a drawer of the desk and placed upon a stack of charts. One of many ink pens is taken from a little basket resting on the window ledge. With this, Oliver composes.

Dearest Elysia,

We have at last come to the apex of our journey. Our blind ambitions have reached too high, and as a result of our unquenchable thirst for the infinite we have breached the limits of the temple. Our very foundations strain and creak, yet still we strive for greater glory. We have become as errant gods.

I need not tell you that a vast tide of destruction is upon us. Ours is a temple built not of human hands, a temple to which we've become so accustomed that we are no longer aware of its presence. That the temple will collapse upon itself is inevitable. There is hope that we may build another, though as yet I can't see how. As precarious as our situation would appear to be, the destruction of the temple seems to be built into its very design. There is hope in that.

I believe that the lodestone may be a key to our salvation, though it could just as easily lead us to the fiery pit. I've gone over the evidence again and again, I've calculated and recalculated, always with the same results. The pieces of this world fit together like those in a Chinese puzzle. I have examined our predicament from every possible angle. There is little possibility of error. I know what I must do.

It is conceivable that we may succeed, as a species, in finding the place in which the celestial cannot be distinguished from the infernal. Those of us who find this place may learn to adapt. That within us which partakes of both natures will allow us to survive what is to come. God help us.

With great urgency, and love,

Joseph S.

The letter is folded and placed in an envelope. On the front of the envelope is written the name and address of a person unknown to Oliver, while in the upper left corner is written an entirely fictitious name and address. Thus with all of Oliver's letters. Each one is made to appear as if it were sent by a different person, none of whom exist, all of which are presumed to live in different parts of the city. Each is mailed to an unsuspecting recipient, chosen through a variety of divinatory methods or at random. The content of the letters reveals the most profound of his thoughts and revelations, without any sort of context or explanation. Aside from whatever perverse pleasure Oliver may derive from this kind of activity, it serves him as an offering to the unknowable, a means by which the course of events may be voluntarily surrendered to processes beyond his understanding or control. It is essential that he leave a space in every aspect of his work by which the invisible may be allowed to manifest. In this way does he court the living spirit of enigma that is to him both as a lover and a god.

The envelope is licked and sealed and a stamp is affixed to the upper right corner. The pouch containing the lodestone is collected, along with a few additional items, all of which are placed into a leather satchel which is then thrown over Oliver's shoulder. He hesitates for but an instant, gazes mournfully about his cramped apartment, and he's off.

The Rites of Bibliomancy

Oliver makes his way down quiet avenues bathed in moonlight as he traverses the streets of the sleeping city. He proceeds from street lamp to street lamp, passing over footbridges and beneath the shadows of high arches. He deftly navigates a stairway below a decorative fountain in a spacious square. By arts at once notorious and revered he has divined the Kabbalistic heart of the city and he would penetrate its vital chambers before the night is through.

The University is a shadow of its former glory. Neglected buildings languish in various states of disrepair, many of them deserted or utilized only for storage. The library, at least, has retained its dignity and purpose. A minor architectural triumph, its curved facade is interspersed with wide doors and windows atop a brief, stepped incline. Before it lies the glory of the Salamander Angel. Naked and sublime, she stands beneath the stars, appearing as an icon of the poetic soul rendered in stone. A thin reptilian tongue darts out from between her lips, while her countenance betrays a mastery of Heaven and Earth. Wings extend outward from her pubic mound. Between them has been delicately carved the letter 'S'. One arm extends above her head, the open palm turned upward toward the sky, while the other points to the regions below. Her limbs and torso, neck and spine, ankles and wrists each betray a letter in some unknown alphabet. Starlight embraces her as if she were a thing not of this Earth. She is an archon of the arcane, an avatar of hidden wisdom.

Oliver lays his leather satchel to one side and opens it up. He removes two brushes, a stack of paper, and a jar of sticky white paste. With meticulous care he slathers the back sides of each sheet of paper with the contents of the jar. These he carries to the two large picture windows that stand on either side of the double doors which serve as the main entrance to the library. He firmly attaches each of them to the glass, one after another, the handwritten text that fills their surfaces well visible beneath the library's outer lights. Oliver has devised an ingenious method of producing an adhesive that cannot be dissolved in water. Once the paste has dried, they will prove quite difficult to remove.

He feels a pang of guilt for defacing such a worthy establishment, but then how better to appease the fallen angels than by a deliberate act of disobedience, a breaking of the social contract? His act of vandalism is nothing less than a type of prayer, an appeal to the unseen ministers of a tradition which by its very nature must remain opaque.

Oliver repeats the process with the remaining pages, covering an appreciable portion of the surface of the windows on either side of the doors. Pains have been taken to give the display a mark of inauthenticity. The pages are slightly crooked and carelessly placed. The paste has been sloppily applied so as to leave drips and streaks across the surface and the text. The job resembles a work of vandalism rather than an official notice.

Next, with paint and brush in hand, he patiently sketches a rough image of the head of Medusa across one of the pairs of doors. Writhing snakes extend beyond the borders of the doorframe, rising up above the pasted pages on either side. The finished image does justice to the Demon Star. With its harsh angles and dripping lines, it is a fitting likeness for the face of desolation. In addition, several figures attributed to Algol are painted on some of the uncovered windows.

Not a second is wasted on the admiration of his handiwork. The lid is pressed back onto the can of paint, the jar of white paste is resealed, and all of his tools are put back into the leather satchel. Oliver takes the single page which has been torn from the surrealistic journal and puts it on the ground before the statue of the Salamander Angel. This he weighs down with a piece of iron. He throws the leather satchel back over his shoulder, and heads back out into the night. The edges of the solitary page flip gently back and forth beneath the meandering fingers of the evening breeze.

✷

Hymn to Algol

Demon Star! Eye of Satan! Ineffable, impenetrable, intolerable Self of the inmost God! How shall we address you, if at all?

In your most secret, silent name: an armed battalion of saints gnaw their tongues in holy ecstasy; a flock of flaming skyscrapers conspire to deflower the sky; alphabets exceed their capacity, contorting into impossible permutations.

You recognize no sacrifice. Your sterility devours its children. You would baffle even the mind of God. O my temptress! O my terror! O invisible sun that shines at midnight! If your inmost chambers are denied us, let us at least behold your outer court. There we will burst into blasphemous flame, hurtling like drunken torches back to our terrestrial abodes. We will be as messengers of the unintelligible, doomed to walk the Earth as burnt-out husks, pariahs in a world of priests.

The echo of the memory of the least traces of your wisdom will sustain us through the procession of the equinoxes. We alone will survive the cataclysmic tides of change, the reversal of the poles, the rotation of the offices of stellar influence. We might at last become your secret martyrs.

O blazing star of heresy! Unpalatable center of austerity! Unattainable gnosis! You have set our very hearts and minds alight with nothing. Let us worship your intangibility. Let us worship your eternal silence. Let us worship even your absence. We who have forgotten your unknowability petition you with lies.

First Excerpt

From *The Sacred Rites of Metallurgy* by W.P. Passante, pages 76-78, found written by hand and pasted upon a window of the university library:

not the only place in which traditions of this type have been observed. The Buriats, a branch of the eastern Mongols, regard the function of the smith or metal-worker as a sacred calling. Their myths include a multifaceted sky god known as Tengri. One particularly compelling story holds that the benevolent aspect of Tengri sent a divine smith, Boshintoj, down to the Earth, along with a daughter and nine sons, to teach the metallurgic arts to humans. You will note the similarities to the myths of the Watchers and the Nephilim of the Old Testament and the apocryphal Book of Enoch, in which a host of angels rebel against the will of their creator, descending into the human world to teach the forbidden arts and sciences. In the Tengri myth, the sons of Boshintoj married earthly women and thus begat the first metal-workers, just as the Watchers were said to have coupled with the daughters of men.

The Buriat smiths perform special rites in which their gods are compelled to protect them against evil spirits. The smithy is considered a sacred house and a place of worship. The sacerdotal craft is handed down from father to son, incorporating initiatory rites and ordeals. Trade techniques are shared like hallowed secrets among exclusive members who are forbidden from revealing them outside of their circle or clan. An aura of sacred mystery surrounds their profession, as if they are partaking in acts coequal with those of the creator.

In ancient Greece and Samothrace we find personages such as the Dactyls and the Korybantes. The Dactyls were known as smiths and magicians in the employ of Hephaestus, the god of blacksmiths and craftsmen. They too taught the arts of metallurgy to humans, along with mathematics and writing. The Korybantes were the guardians of the infant Zeus, and were renowned as metalworkers and seers. Along with the Cabiri and the Telchines, these personages served as the patrons of secret guilds associated both with initiatory mysteries and with the blacksmith's craft. The Cabiri, whose worship was widespread throughout the eastern Mediterranean, were given the title of 'masters of the furnace'. Many of these personages were associated with Cybele, goddess of mountains, mines, and caves.

Not only have those who work with metals been granted a sacred place within society throughout the world, but the metals themselves have been regarded as having otherworldly qualities. The kings of the Malaya would keep a sacred block of iron as part of their regalia. This object was surrounded with an extraordinary veneration mingled with superstitious terror. Throughout northern Europe articles of iron are used as protective talismans against malicious magic and the evil eye. The ancient Romans believed that iron was effective against poisons, and used it as a curative for nocturnal emissions which were thought to deplete the vitalizing essence. Similar beliefs are found in Turkey, Persia, and India.

The alchemists held the metals in a particularly sacred light, claiming that the metallic ores were made to grow within the womb of the Earth by the generative powers of astral emanations shed by the stars. If the alchemist could purify the metal, liberating its root essence from the earthly dross to which it is bound, they would come into possession of no less than the elixir of life.

Nothing has inspired so much awe, or has had such occult power attributed to it throughout the ages, as has meteoric rock. Stones that fall from Heaven enjoy a celestial regard given to nothing of this Earth. Charged with spiritual sanctity, they are taken as an immediate manifestation of the godhead. Ancient accounts tell us that before the stone omphalos was erected at Delphi there was another stone which demarked the oracle as the location of the center of the world, a 'thunderstone' hurled down to Earth by Zeus. A block of meteoric stone stood side by side with Praxiteles' sculptured image of Eros, and was thought to be a direct emanation of the god. The Palladium of Troy was said to have dropped from Heaven, and was adopted as a statue of Athena. The black stone set into the eastern corner of the Ka'aba at Mecca is also said to be of meteoric origin.

Meteoric iron was used by primitive peoples long before they learned to work with ferrous ores. The most ancient term for iron, the Sumerian word 'anbar', is made from the pictograms for 'sky' and 'fire'. According to Cortez, when the Aztec chiefs were asked where they had obtained their knives, they simply pointed at the sky. The kings of the Hittites made frequent use of 'black metal from the sky', as did the Cretans of the Minoan era. The ancient Egyptians, having made no use of iron deposits until the eighteenth dynasty, crafted tools from 'stones of light' which had their origins in

Second Excerpt

From *The Cube, the Stone, and the Heavenly Temple* by René Revante, pages 159-161, found pasted near the pages above:

the Ka'bah to be the precise location of the center of the world. It marked the place where the sacred world intersected with the profane. It is the gateway between Heaven and Earth. Further, the form of the Temple of the Ka'bah is a mirror of the form of the heavenly Throne; that which is below is an image of that which is above.

As has been illustrated in a previous chapter, each of the three worlds is at once the cause of the one below it and its esoteric heart, comprising its hidden center. Likewise, each world is as a flower, while the world above it is the seed from which it blossoms. It is fashionable, in these troubled times, to regard the images shown to us in the inner world as mere symbols of the trials we face throughout the course of our lives. In truth, it is the other way around. It is we ourselves who symbolize Divine processes. Earth is but a mirror of Heaven.

Returning to the writings of the Shiite philosopher, Qadi Sa'id Qummi, we are told that when the pilgrimage is made to Mecca, the heart of the pilgrim is brought into greater accord with the Throne of Heaven. Just as the Celestial Temple is the image of perfection, so is there a temple in the heart which yearns for that perfection. The Temple at Mecca is an image of the heavenly Temple, and through the act of performing the Hajj, the person of faith brings the microcosmic temple in the heart into greater conformity with the macrocosmic Temple in Heaven.

Further, we are told that when this process is set in motion for a single individual, so does each and every person in the kingdom of the world respond invisibly, whether they are of the true faith or not. Thus, every time the pilgrimage is performed, humanity is collectively elevated one step further toward the Throne, the Temples of Heaven and Earth are brought one step closer to reconciliation, and the human world is brought one step closer to the establishment of the earthly paradise.

According to a tradition originating with the sixth Imam, Ja'far al-Sadiq, when God announced the appearance of Adam to the angels, they feared that the Light of the Divine would be concealed from them. The angels thus took refuge around the Throne, circling it in procession for seventy thousand years. God looked with love upon the initiative of the angels, and commanded them to descend to Earth in order to build a temple in the Throne's image. This is the very temple around which Adam and his children performed their circumambulations in imitation of the celestial process.

Another tradition states that the stone of the Ka'bah was once an angel itself, the first to take an oath to agree to a pact with God regarding humanity. Adam's part of the pact was that he keep ever the ways of Heaven. He was required to renew his pact every year before the angel. When he had betrayed the agreement and departed from paradise, he forgot his promise. The angel was then cast out of Heaven, appearing to Adam in the form of a white pearl. When Adam saw the pearl, he remembered the obligation which he'd undertaken. The pearl then became a black stone, and each day and night he renewed his oaths before it. He carried the stone into Arabia, and finally to Mecca, where a temple was erected and the stone embedded in the corner.

Thus, by making the pilgrimage and circumambulating the temple, the pilgrim attunes the stone in his own soul to that of the white pearl, fulfilling his own pact with the Divine which is the condition of his incarnation. When the reconciliation between Heaven and Earth has thus been made complete for any individual, they will have attained to the original state of Adam before he was cast out of paradise.

It should be noted that, just as every individual contains an image of the temple in the heart, so can an image of the temple exist for a community. Thus is every sect which is truly descended from Abraham allotted such an image by which, through the practice of their central rites, the adherents thereof may bring their own inner temple progressively into accord with the heavenly Throne. This can be seen in the Essene community of the Qumran, for instance, particularly in their practice of

Nikolai

Nikolai resides in holy bliss upon one of the elevated rooftops of a complex of buildings near the outskirts of town. Behind the complex runs a railroad track, bordered on the other side by a seemingly endless succession of industrial sites. Further out winds a river which graces one end of the city before continuing southward. The building on which Nikolai is currently standing houses several laboratories used for the development of radar and sonar products.

Nikolai's work begins shortly before the last technician leaves the complex. It is his job to keep the premises secure and to monitor the operation of several devices which must be kept running over long periods. His nightly route is designed to keep him occupied throughout his shift. But Nikolai is clever, and has devised means and techniques whereby his duties may be dramatically reduced. Several tasks have been deemed unnecessary, others have been altered so as to allow him time for idleness and exploration.

More than half of his shift is spent in pursuit of his own designs. Thus he stands now beneath the stars, embraced by the sweet-smelling perfume of night.

Nikolai sits upon the hard black tar and wraps his arms around his knees. His spot commands a satisfactory view of one side of the city, allowing him to keep watch over several areas at once. He watches for nothing in particular. Few can be seen out in the streets at this hour. It gives him great pleasure simply to survey his domain. The empty streets would seem to belong to him and him alone.

He takes a folded letter from a pocket, unfolds it, and places it on the surface of the roof before him, pinning it down with the toe of his boot. He's read through the letter countless times, carefully going over every word, looking for some clue to its possible origin or meaning. It was delivered to him little more than a week before, sent to him, if the name on the return address is to be believed, by an Alexander Konstantinov. The address doesn't seem to exist in his own city or any other. Judging from its contents, it appears to have been written by an insane person. The letter is as delightful as it is perplexing, inspiring just a hint of paranoia. He picks it up and reads through it a final time.

My dear, dear Nikolai,

I realize this letter may come as somewhat of a surprise to you. I beg you not to take any undue concern on my part. I am simply a civil servant carrying out my line of duty as best I can. There is no need to respond.

The fact is, Nikolai, that a great many people have taken an interest in you. There

111

is no threat to your security, mind you, nothing to worry about in that regard. It is simply that you have been identified as a man of fine prospects. We think you will go very far, and we wish for you nothing but the best.

Now, we are faced with a dilemma. A dilemma of unreasonable proportions. We must be held accountable for certain things, things that are, how can I put it? things that are part and parcel of our nature. Do you see what I mean? I don't think that you do.

Here is the issue in a nutshell, Nikolai: we have transgressed the very bounds of our dominion. Not just you and I, of course, but all of us—humanity as a whole. Indeed, our very nature is transgressive. Our bodies have evolved in order to allow us to survive in a particular environment. Our ability to wield tools and to use symbolic values in order to communicate has given us advantages not shared by other species. This has made it possible for us to thrive and to diversify.

And yet, we have used our abilities in ways that they were never intended to be used. We have trespassed into places forbidden to us, found the keys of wisdom hidden behind nature's veil, tricked the guardians of all the thresholds that we might ourselves partake in the very process of creation. We have an unslakeable thirst to taste of fruit that we were never meant to taste, and we have found the means to do so.

Now, it has been suggested that we've been tempted by fallen angels. But were these angels ever anything but ourselves? We would seem to be a race made up of heretics. We rebel against the designs of our creator. We have pried open the doors of the hidden temples and have plundered their inmost treasures. We have profited thereby, and also suffered.

So here we are. And yet again we find ourselves on the threshold of great mysteries. Do we retain our places in the scheme of things? Do we obey the dictates of our natural limitations? I fear that we would not have the ability to do so even were it desirable to us. We must again risk everything in order to rend the veil before us, though in doing so we may incur the wrath of gods long since forgotten. There are those few of us who bear the burden of carrying out our tasks with open eyes, knowing the weight of the ordeals that we bring upon ourselves in doing so. There is a place within each of us, a place hidden within the depths of the soul, where obedience and transgression are as one.

It is up to you, dear Nikolai, to find that place within yourself.

With the greatest respect, and love,

Alexander Konstantinov

What is he to make of such a preposterous contrivance? It seems to him to be nothing less than a holy talisman. Can his idle hands be trusted with the custodianship of such a precious artifact? He is certain that they cannot. The sacred object must be humbly returned to the heart of oblivion, from which it undoubtedly came.

Nikolai takes a battered box of matches from one pocket, removes one of the three remaining match sticks, strikes a flame, and applies it to one corner of the letter. As the flame hops gingerly from match head to letterhead, Nikolai takes the cherished relic with both hands and holds it above his bowed head as if in offering to the moon. Quickly quickly the flames consume the letter, forcing Nikolai to drop the final flaming corner. By the time it nearly reaches the ground, it too has been consumed.

Nikolai is now ready to return to his official patrol. Security cameras line the perimeters of most of the buildings, specifically trained on possible entrances and exits. Nikolai makes sure that he appears with regularity wherever his appointed route takes him within their line of sight. He would rather there be no question as to the proper performance of his job.

He re-enters one of the laboratory commons through an unmonitored skylight. The lights flash on overhead. Had he more time, he might amuse himself by attempting to make it all the way outside of the building without tripping any of the motion detectors. Climbing down upon a filing cabinet, he jumps to the floor and heads out through a pair of white double doors. A short trip down the hallway leads to a rickety freight elevator. Nikolai slides his passkey through the slot, presses the button, and waits. It would be quicker to take the stairs, but he finds the mechanical creaks and groans produced by the operation of the freight elevator to be particularly delightful.

At length, the elevator doors wheeze open as if they barely contain the strength to carry out their line of duty. Nikolai boards, and after a quick trip down to the next level he emerges into the shelter of a loading dock. A security camera observes him making his rounds exactly at the time expected, as if he were bound to anything but the dictates of his heart.

From the loading dock, Nikolai dutifully paces from checkpoint to checkpoint, assuring himself that all areas are secured. In the three years that he's worked for the company, there has never once been a single break-in. He quickly completes his circumambulation, regaining entrance to the sacred temple through a monitored security door around the back by the train tracks. The tracks are separated from the complex by a chain-link fence, followed by a small depression covered in brambles. Nikolai has created a hidden breach in the fence, through which a short path may be taken to a metallic platform that rises above the tracks. He often leans against the rail of the platform and watches as the trains go by beneath him, having long since memorized their schedules. Forgoing such luxuries for the moment, he heads back to the roof, stopping first in one of the offices to pick up a pair of binoculars.

One of the great pleasures of Nikolai's life is watching people who do not think that they are being watched. He has no desire to invade anybody's privacy, he shudders at the thought of watching people in their homes, but there's something about watching people go about their business that he finds endlessly fascinating. Thus are the long hours of the night idly whiled away.

To his great delight, there would seem to be a man meandering his way through the city streets at this very moment. This is no idle wanderer, indeed the man is striding with the surety of intent. Nikolai watches through the binoculars. A pair of spectacles rests beneath a balding pate. A worn leather satchel is crossed over the chest, hung from one shoulder. The man would appear to know exactly where he's going. With determination he proceeds along a clearly pre-planned route. Nikolai follows the man for a few minutes as he traverses an open square and scuttles down a staircase in one of the commercial districts. Where could he be going? At length, the tiny man disappears down a narrow street which is hidden from Nikolai's view.

He lowers the binoculars, shifting his gaze over to a row of small buildings several blocks away. Occasionally, he manages to catch a janitor moving about from office to office, visible through a consecutive series of windows, emptying garbage cans or dusting the surfaces of desks and doorframes. He maintains some small hope of catching a fellow night worker at leisure, relaxing on one of the leather couches in some office, or riffling through the drawers of a desk. It baffles him that he has never once observed this. Could it be possible that he's unique in his poor work habits? He can't imagine that the janitors in all of the buildings that can be seen from his rooftop spend the entirety of their shifts engaged in honest work. Or are they simply more careful than he is, relaxing only when they're sure they can't be seen?

Nikolai heads down to the southern wing of the complex, replacing the binoculars on the way. He passes by a modest scientific library, filled with books and periodicals used by the technicians and researchers in their work. Nikolai has become increasingly fascinated with the technologies which are researched and developed by the company. He's spent countless hours in the sonar labs, fiddling about with working models of newly developed imaging devices, examining complex testing apparatus, logging onto the single computer for which he's managed to find the credentials and scrutinizing half-finished documentation and development logs.

His mystic sensibilities are stimulated by the operations of the curious machines. The creation of topographical maps beneath the surface of the sea, the probing of the ocean floor with invisible signals, the transmission and reception of pulsations in order to determine such vagaries as depth and pressure; all of this would seem to him to recall the forgotten divinatory rites of ancient civilizations. There is something of the essential, so he feels, about these practices.

Part of Nikolai's job is to monitor several banks of oscilloscopes and pulse analyzers throughout the complex. These are attached to experimental radar models which line one of the rooftops on which Nikolai would never dare set foot. Signals are sent from a series of transmitters placed strategically about the city, while the devices test the receiving capabilities of the radars, checking for signal to noise ratios and other such diagnostics. Occasionally one of the devices will crash and will have to be rebooted in order to avoid large gaps in the collection of data.

Entering the radar lab, Nikolai switches off the lights. Several monochrome displays present a wide variety of electronic readouts: circular sweeps chart blips within a particular range, beta scans track signals against distance markers, wavy lines of light march left to right across convex circular panels set within houses of thick plastic. Starlight streams in through a dusty bank of windows above, dimly illuminating the flaking flat-blue paint on the walls. A coffeemaker sits on the corner of one table, plugged into a surge protector shared by several plugs of every shape and variety. A little red light shines from above the pot, indicating that a fresh pot has recently been brewed. Nikolai pours himself a cup and sits down in a swivel chair before the faint glow of the machines. He sits and sips his coffee in blessed solitude as time stands still.

Nikolai's dull reverie is broken by a number of anomalous signals which appear all at once on the faces of several of the devices. Sine waves contract, spectrum analyzers distort, and several oscillators indicate an unexpected ratio of noise to signal. Swiftly the noise increases as quiet beeps give way to static bursts. Nikolai rises from his chair, perplexed. Is it an atmospheric disturbance? A flock of birds congregating around the transmitters or receivers? A misdirected signal jammer? He supposes he'd better go up to the roof and see if he can spot anything unusual.

He makes his way up to his cherished spot, where the receiving dishes can be seen just a few rooftops over. Nothing seems to be interfering with them. He checks those few of the transmission devices which are visible from the rooftop and sees nothing which would indicate any disturbance. The source of the disruption would seem to be a mystery, some unseen signal pulsing through the abysses of the city.

Nikolai walks to the edge of the building and gazes out over the surrounding blocks. Sleeping windows contentedly sigh from their confines of brick and plaster. He stands serene beneath the voluptuous dome of the firmament. A light breeze tumbles across the rooftops, bathing the shadows in the hushed breath of starlight. The sky holds the city in holy embrace as innumerable angels surrender to the heart of Heaven.

The Hidden Church

The ceremony has begun. The flames of carefully arranged candles flick and shimmer like the facets of a gnostic gem. Consecrations, banishings, purifications, and litanies have been duly performed. It is all very momentous. Simon swings a censer in an arc which perfectly describes the measurements of the Temple of Solomon. Sweet-smelling smoke assails the circle, winding its tendrils gently around the furniture thereof. Unit, meanwhile, holds the center, one arm raised and clutching a lamp, the other covering the nether regions of her body. She is the axis mundi, the keeper of the hidden light, the means by which the theurgist may ascend into the holy temple of the Mysteries.

Preliminary prayers are recited, gifts are offered to the guardians of the gates, the liquor is ceremoniously poured; the temple has been opened in the name of the unnamable. The lamp is placed upon the ground to seal the entrance to the holy place. Simon, having divested himself of censer, gives a sign of supplication as Unit rhythmically strikes a bell. The invocation of the Salamander Angel may begin.

Unit's invocation has been carefully constructed over the preceding weeks, incorporating formulas and motifs that she's developed over years of practice. The qualities of the angel invoked are poetically recited along with various names by which she's known in diverse traditions. Her virtues are extoled. She is praised and worshipped. Blessings are offered to her secret church, perpetuated invisibly throughout the ages. Its anonymous saints are honored in rhymed couplets. Sigils are traced in the air, visualized in colored flame. Supplementary divinities are invoked.

Simon remains seated, mute and imperious, occasionally throwing bits of resin on the charcoal. With each phase of the invocation, the phrasing grows more outlandish, the gestures more erratic, all working up to an ecstatic climax. Their performance is every bit an elaborate production, as if the inhabitants of the exalted regions can't be bothered with anything less than an all-out assault on the veil of the threshold of Heaven.

But let us leave them for a time. Let us turn out attention elsewhere. Let us return to Peter in the astral vision of the desecrated church.

The walls of this church would appear to be made of light, as would the floor and ceiling, pews and carpets, doors and windows, alcoves and archways, as well as the pedestals on which stand living icons of forces unknown to the coarser of the senses. All is as it was before. Where once a rotting altar stood is now an ornate stand of stunning white marble. The once moldy carpet now reveals intricate designs concealing parabolic messengers and cherubs in the form of fleurs-de-lis. White pillars flank whispering inlets. The pews are all arranged as if for Sunday service. The space is lit without candles. The shadows have been banished. Night has been forgotten in this holy place.

The angelic statue that had so enchanted Peter earlier stands arched with sublime dignity above the altar, wings extended further than her body could be reasonably expected to support. She is the heart of the church, the sacred flame within the temple, the rose upon the cross.

Upon the altar sits a book. It is a massive tome, containing the secret and holy name by which the church is known in the angelic tongue, written out in endless parables replete with digressions and accompanied by explanatory diagrams. Or so one might assume given the grandiosity of its design. It is bound in brilliant white cloth with gold fittings on the corners and soft brown leather spine. There is an image, a sort of silhouette in bright red, embossed upon the cover.

Peter drifts before the altar, swiftly without movement of the feet, as vague echoes suggestive of a distant chorus waft through the hidden church like clouds of incense. The image on the book is that of an iconic salamander. Has Peter seen this image anywhere before? He doesn't quite recall.

The book is opened. An illustration set within a thick black border is revealed. It is an image of great wonder, revealing what must be thousands of winged figures, some dressed as monarchs, others as mendicants, some bearing weapons, others such items as keys, scepters, lilies, or spyglasses, some appearing saintly with long beards, others fraught with holy rage, all of them awhirl in a kaleidoscopic moiré around the tremendous figure of a cube. An infinity of dark azure surrounds the scene, which, though the whole is contained within the confines of the page, appears in a colossal aspect. What's more, the image appears to be in motion. Endless wings beat syncopated rhythms in the air as folds of robes unfurl and fluctuate with maddening vivacity. Countless bodies trace paths defining unacceptable geometries. It's as if the page were a window looking out onto the drama of creation from a place of honor in the inner court of Heaven.

Peter is no stranger to the exaggerated richness of the subtle planes. It is not unusual for archetypal images to present themselves to the inner eye in a numinous light that appears much larger than life. Thus the mind responds when confronted with anything greater than itself. Dramatic reenactments of the mysteries of creation unfold with startling consistency in the life of the visionary. This notwithstanding, our seer and explorer is delighted and surprised at the sight of the tableau revealed to him. It is not what he expected. There would appear to be something of importance to the history of this church that is not obvious from outward appearance, and this something has left its mark upon the astral substance of the place.

Peter turns the page of the book. The second plate reveals a wholly different scene. The inside of a church is shown, not unlike the one in which Peter now finds himself. Angels of annunciation surround the altar, four of them, each bearing a trumpet partially enwrapped in a length of parchment which unfolds before it. Their wings extend to the limits of the church. The angels appear very authoritative, even grave. Upon the altar is a black stone.

The parchments have phrases written on them, just discernable to Peter if he focuses his attention on one or another. On the first, behind the altar and to the left, appears the phrase *Lapis Lapsus ex Coelis*. On the second, to the other side of the altar, is printed a single word: *Shatiya*. The third, before and to the left of the altar, reads

Omphalos, while the phrase on the fourth is *Lapsit Exillis*. The angels raise their trumpets. The voices of the brass burst forth in a portentous wail which quickly ascends to a crescendo, at the very peak of which the page curls up on its own and flips back down on the other side, revealing the next illustrated plate.

The scene now revealed is one of havoc and destruction. The church is in flames. The roof has been consumed and the annunciating angels have retreated to the corners of the sky. The fire rages and whirls about the altar in a vicious torrent of violent annihilation. A single star shines brightly from above. Its trenchant rays cut through the smoke-filled atmosphere like diamonds, penetrating into the secret recesses of the destroyed church. Peter looks upon the mayhem and disorder from the midst thereof, for he is now inside the scene. The book is nowhere to be found. In its place upon the altar resides the black stone, stark and austere, directly below the blazing star. The angels again lift their trumpets. The majestic chorus has become a cacophony, as if the howls of the damned were echoing back and forth across the sky. The unholy annunciation again shrieks forth, cracking the very firmament as heavy black smoke closes in from all directions.

And suddenly a wave of darkness consumes the scene, followed by a rolling revelation of the scene to come. The earth has opened up beneath Peter's feet and has swallowed the remains of the church. Splintered wood and stained glass hurtle downward through an endless sea of rolling flame and treacherous black rock. Peter follows, voluntarily or not, plunging into the smoking, seething world below. The hallowed halls of Tartarus receive him as if he'd long since been a member. The hosts of the infernal monarch dart in and out of towering walls of fire. Monuments of malice and dismay protrude from spires of crumbling stone at intolerable angles. Thick atrocities of soot curl upward from a sulfurous landscape below.

Stationed immobile in the center of perdition sits the altar of white marble, a beacon of purity in the midst of the wretched blight on the floor of Gehenna. On it is the black stone, naked and resplendent.

For a moment it is as if the scene is frozen. The stone exerts a fascination that cannot quite be defined. There is a sense of remembrance, as if Peter were looking upon his own face, yet before it had come to develop any distinguishing features. All at once, as if smacked by a seraph, Peter is thrown back with tremendous force and sent hurtling through the flames. He passes through a ring of darkness only to find himself flung back into the center of the church. There is no smoke, no chaos, no flames or splintered wood. The church is as it was, holy and sublime, bathed in the luminous essence of the blessed. The angel stands again above the altar with hands cupped and wings outspread. The heavy white book slams shut as if it were never meant to be opened.

The Infernal Throne

The light of the stars shining forth from their celestial abodes is carried down into the streets on unfeeling currents as Oliver navigates a circuitous maze of tenement buildings in various states of disrepair. The university with its library is far from him now. The carefully preserved environments of the old town have been left behind, giving way first to the new construction of the soviet era, and further still to more disreputable quarters of the city. Venerable monuments to culture and industry drift by, keeping watch over the sleeping streets. The residential is gradually superseded by the industrial, which itself grows sparse as the periphery of the city approaches.

Oliver moves through the streets as if pulled by some magnetic influence. The lodestone which he carries in his satchel vibrates in accordance with the fevered pitch of the night. The stars pulse and flicker from their houses in the firmament, bearing ominous imperatives to the habitations of the sleeping. Telluric tides pulse through infernal mansions as angelic dignitaries collaborate in nocturnal conspiracies never to be divined by man.

Oliver crosses over the train tracks near the western border of the city as he heads toward the river. Spanned on the northern end by an impressive aqueduct and further south by several small bridges, the river's banks can be reached by following any number of possible routes through the more desolate end of town. Oliver notices fresh footsteps in the mud as he approaches the edge of the water. Somebody else has been here this very night. Perhaps some vagrant, come to bath himself or to satisfy his thirst.

Oliver looks up at the sky. The pole star glares down from the extreme north of the heavens. Solitary, distant, and compassionless, a fitting icon for the icy desolation of the arctic wastes. It is written that a region of unendurable darkness awaits the spiritual traveler on the approach to the celestial pole. According to the sages, this is not darkness at all, but light of such fineness that it cannot be perceived as such. It is light without reflection. Who would approach this light must be prepared for the annihilation of the sense of self; for when the soul is made perfect, it sees nothing but God.

South of the celestial axis, in the constellation of Perseus, shines the star most despised by ancient astrologers. This is precisely the one whose emanations Oliver wishes to attract. He wades into the river a short distance, positioning himself before the reflection of the maligned star, which is only barely visible on the surface of the water. The pouch containing the lodestone is retrieved from his satchel, and the lodestone itself removed. O blessed stone of unknown origin! O sacred relic of the axis spanning Earth and Heaven! He gently lowers the stone into the waters in the place where the star's light is reflected. Does the angel of the lodestone sanctify the operation? Is there a subtle shift in the procession of the Seraphim around the Holy Throne? Oliver delivers the stone back from beneath the waters and into his little pouch, which is then put back into the satchel.

Marita, at this very moment, is now in the heart of the city. She follows ancient routes from quarter to quarter, bearing ever the light invisible before her like some initiatory guide. She traverses streets and avenues of which the venerable names have long since been forgotten. She vibrates in sympathy with the rich, dark minerals beneath the earth and the endless expanse of the heavens. Up a wide stairway she goes, coming at last before the statue of the Salamander Angel. This she anoints with a substance or an essence neither wholly one nor the other. Then she is off again.

Just a short distance from the library, in a little apartment tucked into a mausoleum for the living, the Salamander Angel has descended in spirit into the consecrated vessel of Unit's body. Time and time again has Unit given herself to ancient gods and their attendant angels, allowing them to speak with her voice while she remains lost in the exalted consciousness of the god invoked. She remains aware of her surroundings, to be sure. She doesn't give up control entirely. Rather there is a sort of split in her awareness; she maintains a minimal control of her physical vehicle while looking through the eyes of the divinity. As such, the earthly and visionary worlds are superimposed one onto the other.

Thus, the Salamander Angel contemplates a majestic temple of stellar proportions. Walls of ivory rise on all sides, covered with coral lattice work inset with lapis lazuli, emerald, and jasper. Winged holy living creatures whirl around the temple in perplexing geometric patterns. Altars of brass host flaming figurations of wonder and beauty the likes of which the Earth has never known.

"The vault of Heaven has been breached!" so speaks the Salamander Angel through Unit's tongue. "The celestial throne has been abandoned! The angels have forsaken the place of paradise! The fruit of immortality has been thrust into the center of the Earth!"

Simon scribbles furiously, trying his damnedest to record every word.

"The gates of Hell have opened for the celestial monarch. Thus will they remain forever. The damned will be redeemed, for there is no sin upon the earth or under the earth. Embrace them! Turn them not away from your abodes and habitations! They come bearing gifts which you will accept with gladdened hearts.

"A new flame alights also in the temple at the height of the axis, but who shall know it? It will appear inscrutable, an abomination; whoso beholds it will think the throne has become desolate, an infinitude of emptiness.

"But there is a treasure as yet uncalculated. Your gold shall be as dust, your silver as the filth upon the earth, your precious stones will be cast into the sea once you've divined the worth of the new coin of Heaven. Now it is unknown to you. Will you be poor in spirit?

"Come then before me, naked and ashamed, cursed, lost, and damned, and I will give to you a key. Keep it in a place unknown to you. Though you be reduced to ashes, there it will remain throughout eternity.

"Now give yourself to the exiled and the wretched, seek them out and pronounce their names. There will be a consummation of the marriage of the sacred and the profane. You will set foot in unexpected places. There is a place for you unsought, a secret place kept inviolate throughout the ages. This will be your home.

"The east has been forsaken. Align your temples to the north. Renounce your holy vows, for the veils have been cast down! The strongholds of the mighty have fallen! The unutterable word has been revealed!"

Unit hits the floor, which simply doesn't happen in the usual course of events. Her body lies limp before the altar. Simon jumps up unthinking, as much from shock as to provide some sort of aid. As soon as he's on his feet his inner vision is flooded with an image of unwavering conviction. A black throne stands stark with depravity and utter desolation. A host of infernal angels circumambulate its base while the howls of a million tortured souls soak the atmosphere in scarlet waves of encroaching terror. Figures insensible are carved into the throne, revealing the basest and most primitive expressions of the nullity of primal mind. An involuntary wail rises from the back of Simon's throat while Unit remains supine.

His cry is drowned out by the unyielding thunder of a deafening blast. The Salamander Angel—it must be She!—stands towering above the throne with a trumpet to her lips. The roar of pandemonium rises in pitch until the vision can no longer be sustained and all is shattered like the windows of a cathedral in an air raid.

Algol

There would seem to be a great commotion stirring in the heavens. There is contention among the Thrones and Principalities, a disturbance in the very House of God. An unfathomable tension grips the atmosphere as the entrances to the forbidden places are exposed. But let us set aside these tempestuous perturbations for a time. We must try and compose ourselves, for there is more to come. We must not forget Peter, after all.

Peter stands on luminous feet within the astral emanations of the holy place. The roof above his head seems to have disappeared, leaving him exposed to a night sky speckled with stars. He stands facing the altar beneath the angel, rows of pristine pews to either side. The bluish-white glow of the heavens descends upon the hushed abode like a blessing from the mantle of The Prophet.

The sacred atmosphere abruptly shifts as Peter becomes aware of a single star positioned directly above the church, a radiant luminary which outshines all the others. This would not appear to be a herald of celestial benevolence. Rather, its penetrating brilliance exudes a devastating sense of malice. It emanates an intolerable light, evincing a profound indifference to all things soever. It is a horror to behold.

As if in response to the appearance of the malevolent star, the figures on the pedestals come to life. One after another, they step forward from their habitations in the niches along the walls. They march in unison to the center of the church where they fall in line, pivot together, and proceed directly above Peter's head toward the angel above the altar. They spread out in a semi-circle directly before the blessed icon. Each one inserts a hand into their robe, withdrawing from the folds therein an elaborately decorated dagger. The blades are raised into the air above their heads, each gleaming in the baneful light. The scene hangs frozen for a moment as Peter's heart leaps into his throat. The figures bring their blades sharply down, each violating the sanctity of their own bodies in a different place. The first figure draws the knife across his throat, the second plunges it into his heart, the next blade is twisted deep into the belly, while the fourth figure stabs the flesh of one wrist and pulls the knife along the forearm to the inside of the elbow. Thick, red blood spurts forth from all four wounds at once, collecting in the angels' waiting hands. Not a single drop is spilled from her cupped palms; not a splash upon the altar, nor a dribble to the floor below. Once the shallow basin has been filled with blood, the four figures collapse before the altar, leaving little more than a mound of crumpled robes.

Peter stands alone before the angel. Her gaze shifts to meet his own. She addresses him directly, breaking her silence for the first time since the vision began. "Who will now occupy the throne of Hell?" she demands in an exacting voice.

Of course, poor Peter cannot answer. He doesn't have the slightest clue what's going on. He simply gives a sign of silence and lets himself sink down through the gates of light and back into his body which awaits him in the musty environment of the decaying church. The vision has come to an end.

Peter opens his physical eyes to see another man staring back at him in the darkness. Startled, he jumps to his feet and takes a few steps back. He finds himself frozen, unable to move for the tension which wracks his body as a result of the unexpected encounter. There is a taut stand-off. Neither of the men are quite able to ascertain whether or not the other constitutes a threat. Their gazes remain locked, each waiting for the other to make a move or to offer a word of explanation. Tense seconds pass. Peter tries not to let his eyes give away his intentions. The other man is standing between him and his means of escape. He notices that the man's clothes are soaking wet. There is some hope that this might act as an impediment in the event of a chase. Deciding to chance it, Peter breaks into a run, darting past the man and scrambling back up to the empty window. Oliver lets himself relax as Peter makes his exit, glad to have avoided a confrontation.

Alone now in the church, Oliver turns to face the statue of the angel. Her cupped hands beckon to him. The star Algol shines through the empty circular window above from its place in the heavens. He takes the pouch from his satchel and removes the stone. It glistens in the faint starlight. He turns it over in his fingers, nurturing a hint of doubt. The weight of the cold, wet rock gently guides his attention to the physicality of his surroundings. The church may once have been quite lofty in its modest way, but now it is in utter ruin. Shafts of dim light shining in through small holes in the roof play over a catastrophe of mold and rot. The furniture is in disarray. The statuary is crumbling and decrepit. The musty odor of the place is almost unbearable.

Oliver approaches the altar. Hesitatingly, so as not to collapse with it onto the filthy concrete, he lifts himself up onto its base, tentatively rising to a crouching position. The altar remains fixed in place. Oliver lets himself stand upright, keeping his arms slightly extended for balance. Once he is secure, he looks up at the majestic figure looming above him, carefully estimating his ability to reach his goal. Stretching both arms upward, he gently grabs hold of the rough, stone hands of the angel, taking great care not to pull the statue down on top of him. Using his thumb to push the stone between two fingers, he is just able to persuade it to roll over the lip formed by the sides of the hands, where it then rolls down into the basin of the bowl formed by her palms.

He quickly scrambles back down from the altar and takes a few steps back. He waits a moment in anticipation of he knows not what. No thunderous crack resounds throughout the church. There is no ethereal light, nor penetrating voice issuing forth from Heaven or from Hell. The church remains as it was, shot through with the sublime grotesquery of decay.

He waits there for a moment, uncertain, yet without disappointment. It's not as if he had expected any visible change to take place before him. He takes a few more steps back, removes his spectacles and polishes them with his shirt, puts them back upon his face and looks about, hesitates again, turns, and leaves the church.

Apotheosis

We have made it through to the end of the night, the final hour before the light returns and a new day begins. The city prepares itself for the catastrophe of sunrise. Birdsong cracks the silence which has held the city hostage through the bleaker hours. Here and there a window opens and the sound of percolating coffee can be heard. Serenity pervades the streets like mist. There is a barely perceptible light in the sky.

Two aged theology professors stroll along a desolate boulevard, Professor Sokal and Professor Angelov, each thoroughly ensconced in the world of academia. They are on their way to the University, where they will sit on a public bench before one of the administrative buildings and indulge in the lost arts of deliberation and debate as the sun emerges from its nightly sojourn through the house of ill repute. Each of them carries a little snifter half-full of brandy, not strictly legal, but then who is there to accost them at this hour? Besides, they're only old professors, nobody pays them any mind.

Already they find themselves engrossed in heated conversation. It would seem that some new upstart has been publishing articles in various journals. Articles which contain controversial views. While the new perspectives espoused are not entirely without merit, Professor Sokal finds the expositions as a whole to be a little premature. "His work is poorly researched, I'm afraid," he swirls his brandy as he walks. "His thesis is made irrelevant by his failure to correctly discern the greater alchemical stone from the lesser in several instances. He's failed to understand Edinger's commentaries on the Pythagorean Tetractys in regard to the progression of the stages of the work. The same short-sightedness is applied to the relation between the lesser and greater mysteries at Eleusis. To compare the two without an appreciation of the ratio between them is to ignore the crucial thread that runs throughout the mysteries of the ages, the precise relation between Heaven and Earth. It is this relation which, as Edinger so eloquently points out in his *Quaternio Lectures*, defines no less than the course of the evolution of the soul."

"This won't stop our young professor from rising through the ranks of academia." Professor Angelov walks with one hand enveloped in a jacket pocket, while the other holds his brandy steadily before him. "His work is receiving favorable reviews. You know as well as I do that the traditionalist approach has long since fallen out of favor."

"Well, he won't be invited to speak at Eranos, I'll tell you that much."

"Nobody cares about Eranos anymore. Alas, my friend, our time has passed. We would do well to simply lie down and accept it."

"Bah! Our work is merely going underground, as must happen from time to time. It's a necessary transition, part of a recurring cycle." Professor Sokal pauses briefly to take a sip of brandy. "It is this very going underground which will allow these views to perpetuate. They must occasionally fall out of the public spotlight in order to regenerate in a changed world. The world needs us now more than ever. It's we who have the job of keeping the torches lit during our passage through the dark."

"So you maintain. I'm not convinced that these ideas require anything from us. Truth will endure with or without our help."

The two professors pass by the opera house with its stately pillars and iron balconettes. Proud testaments to the triumph of the arts and sciences line the wide boulevards that head off in several directions. They pass the church of Saint Abadios before traversing the spacious Republic Square in silence. Before long they approach the University itself.

"Now it is well known," Professor Sokal asserts unprompted, "that the Western world is in the grip of nothing less than a full-scale ontological crisis. It would seem that our God has forsaken us, if ever there was a God at all. But even God evolves, do you see? Or, at the very least, our conception of what God must be evolves. Whether or not there is a God is immaterial—it is our attitude, collectively, toward the idea of God that shapes every aspect of our culture."

"And if God is forgotten completely?"

"Even so, if we abandon the sacred in the name of science, or whatever it is we choose to enthrone in its place, if even the very concept of God is eradicated from the face of the world, that is itself a means of regarding the ineffable, and will show itself as such in time. The human psyche cannot exist without some concept of a greater perfection. It is a feature of the mind itself."

"Some would say that it's a flaw in the design," says Angelov. "You can't deny that our world is finding less and less of a place for the holy."

"This I can't deny," agrees Sokal. "I suspect we are witnessing the early stages of the fall of religion as we know it. And yet, I absolutely maintain that the Divine will make itself known to us through the very architecture of our collective nihilism. The worldview of the atheist is nothing but another mask of God. Even the existentialist finds Divinity in the meaninglessness of existence, though they may not recognize it as such."

"You are a hopeless romantic, Gerhard. You really ought to have been a poet. I can't help but think that your views are nothing so much as a bunch of fanciful words. What difference does it make to the melancholic, for instance, if you tell them that their very melancholy—hold on! What the devil has gone on at the library?"

"What are you on about? Oh, would you look at that! Vandals!"

"Who in their right mind would deface a library?"

"The city's given birth to a whole new breed of degenerate," exclaims Sokal in disgust. "They respond to culture as though it were a threat. Of course they haven't an inkling of what we've been through in the decades before they were born. They think themselves invulnerable, I'd imagine."

"Ah, well. I suppose it's best just to leave it be," sighs Angelov. "The young will strike out at anything within reach. Anyway, it's just some paint and glue and paper. Nothing a good day's work won't repair."

"I can't see why they wouldn't vandalize a bank instead," grumbles Sokal before finishing his brandy, "or even a government office."

"Our library has no security cameras," Angelov points out. "In any case, I wouldn't think that this is an act of targeted aggression. The perpetrators were probably just out for a bit of fun."

The two gentlemen continue on their way, happy to find themselves again in the familiar embrace of the University. The gorgon's impenetrable gaze would seem to have moved elsewhere; she no longer shines her abysmal influence upon the hallowed halls of learning. The faint gleam of the Greater Dog Star is now just visible in the lightening skies above.

In another place within the city, Peter meanders through the urban labyrinth, heading back to his little flat in the eastern side of town. There he will make an entry in the latest of a stack of leather-bound journals in which he logs every one of his nocturnal adventures in meticulous detail. He's managed to amass a rich body of work over the years. This morning's entry will be especially compelling. The church will have to be sketched and diagramed, its splendors rendered from several different views. The features of the physical church will be carefully compared to those of the astral, taking into account also the layout of the church as it appeared within the pages of the book upon the altar. Nothing fascinates Peter so much as the architecture of the invisible. One might derive an encyclopedic reference book on visionary cartography from the voluminous depths of his journals. His explorations of the hidden recesses of the city, from the heart of the small kingdom to its bowels, have revealed a treasure house of mystery and wonder unknown to any but himself, of which tonight's excavation may well be the most extravagant jewel.

Yet further on, following routes now known to us, we come to a modest inner-city alleyway, where, behind the iron bars of a cramped balcony, Unit allows Simon to lie in her arms as they share a final cigarette for the night. Simon is still visibly shaking, his fragile ego somewhat shattered. Unit has little patience for any kind of frailty, but in this case she restrains her contempt. She understands that it is necessary for him to pass through all the agonies of purgation. He has set foot where he was not prepared to go, not by virtue of excessive valor or temerity, but simply because he could not have known where he was going.

In the decade or so during which they've worked together, Unit has taken pains to ensure that Simon is not faced with anything too far beyond his depth. The same cautions have not been taken for herself. She's pitched herself headfirst into unfathomable waters often enough to have attained a degree of comfort with the experience of drowning. It's easier for her. She has a natural emptiness inside which renders her impervious to loss. She knows that the desolation of her own abysses conceals a greater fullness, and it is precisely in this seeming nothingness that she finds nourishment. Simon is still somewhat of a child in that regard. His innocence has thus far protected him, but tonight he's been deflowered. He will not understand the nature of the changes which will overcome him in the coming weeks; he's never tasted so deeply of these fruits before. It will be for him a terrible ordeal. He will be made to face the uncompromising austerity of the soul stripped naked.

Whatever changes lie ahead for Simon, she feels certain that for all intents and purposes their relationship will remain exactly as it is. The most profound of transformations so often fail to produce any visible changes at all. The world of appearances cannot compete with the invisible; it would constitute a sort of blasphemy for it to try.

At last, we come to Oliver. He has returned to his apartment, where he now looks mournfully upon his empty humidor. His work is complete and there is little left to do. To be sure, there will be other lines of investigation. He'll continue to send papers to obscure theosophical journals, maybe even write a book or two, but for the moment he feels rather empty, as if he's reached the highest point of what has passed for a career and yet has nothing to show for it. Whether or not his work has been relevant to anything outside of the machinations of an overactive mind he'll never know, though he supposes it hardly matters. He has long cultivated the habit of pursuing his studies for their own sake, as if they were an art form and he an artist striving for perfection.

He begins the odious task of gathering up the mess of charts and tables and densely illustrated texts which lie strewn across his crowded desk. Before long, exhaustion overtakes him and he decides to leave the task for the following day. He closes the lid of the humidor, drags his drooping body to a small mattress in one corner of the room, curls up, and goes to sleep.

Marita

Quiet rapture hangs frozen in dawn's early light as the city awakes. Alarms go off, a thousand thousand sleepers stir. Coffee brews and toast is buttered. The residents go out from their houses and apartments and take to the streets, catching rides on trolleys and busses, driving automobiles along crowded boulevards, walking swiftly down footpaths, unlocking office doors and taking phone calls. Morning meetings are held. Figures are affirmed. The clacking of the keys of countless keyboards can be heard reverberating from the open windows of every enterprise within the city limits. People go about their business, embracing the day as if it is no different from any other.

Hustling crowds of assiduous workers trace well-established paths through passages brought to life with the rising of the sun, each and every individual endowed with a force of motion and intention undivinable to any casual observer. Flashing traffic lights conduct enigmas unfathomable amidst the steady rhythm of pedestrian feet. Shopkeepers and construction workers enact Masonic mysteries in well-lit temples, uttering coded phrases and displaying obfuscated icons against a backdrop of perplexing harmonies and discords. The sun is risen, the veil of night has been pulled back, the madness of the day is set in motion and nothing in Heaven or Earth can alter its course.

In some uncared for quarter of the city, away from the attentions of the industrious and unsuspecting masses, Marita has found her way inside the hidden church. The presence of the star exalted in her breast has activated the magnetic lodestone. The celestial has been brought into the place of the infernal. The church, and thus the city, has been made like unto her. The work is now complete. A new dawn alights upon the city. We march as yet unseeing toward the sky, the heavenly abode, the stars themselves.

A Book of Alabaster

STEFAN lived alone in the lookout tower. Like a beacon of austerity it stood, looming above the pallid suburban landscape, an affront to the homogenous aesthetic embraced by the neighborhood. The tower sat perched atop a house of no great distinction. Once owned by a notorious eccentric who built the imposing minaret in the final years of his declining health, the property was inherited by a nephew who himself occupied only the lower quarters. Stefan paid a modest monthly rate for the distinction of living in what was generally considered to be a blight upon the neighborhood.

But he loved his tower. It suited him. Stefan was a solitary figure, frequently staying up throughout the unspeakable hours of the night to pore over his collection of rare books and precious artifacts. On warm nights, he could be found sitting atop the platform which comprised the roof of his home, sipping a glass of Malbec as he read exquisite poetry beneath the stars. He felt like a monarch in his cloistered citadel. He entertained few visitors. He was the very model of self-sufficiency.

The upper story was attainable only through a staircase which ran along one side of the house before disappearing into the base of the tower. From there it spiraled upward, increasingly tightening its arc until it opened out into a spacious room surrounded on all sides by windows. Stefan allowed just a hint of opulence to grace the minimal décor of the upper apartment. Furniture was sparse, bookshelves were many, the latter lined with precious volumes artfully arranged and interspersed with a pleasing variety of curious devices. Three shelves placed sequentially divided the space into two distinctly separate areas. A little ladder extended along one window to a hatch leading to the roof. The whole space was thoroughly unique, cozy, and remote.

Stefan was pleased when the package arrived in the mail. It came unadorned and inconspicuous; the envelope had no return address. Inside was a cartridge, a game for a somewhat antiquated home entertainment system. He'd found it advertised in an online forum in some obscure corner of the electronic market after fruitless weeks of searching. He'd taken a chance, sending money to a pseudonymous seller using an anonymous payment service, never knowing whether or not he'd receive his order. It was a trivial risk; the game was not expensive. Nevertheless, he was quite excited to have finally received it.

It had occurred to him one day, apropos of nothing, that he would enjoy revisiting what had doubtless been the most treasured possession of his childhood. Fond memories of the game flitted through Stefan's mental landscape like scattered sunlight shining through the crowns of birches in an autumn dawn. He remembered in particular the sense of mystery that had attended it, and the allure of open-ended exploration which promised no end of arcane delights and inexplicable discoveries. Nor did it fail to deliver on its promises; countless hours of play were frequently rewarded with the most perplexing revelations. The feeling he had most cherished was that which resulted whenever a new area was found within the game. The landscape consistently surprised him, subverting his expectations with each new addition to its ever expanding map; and yet there was always a sense of recognition, as if the game had somehow revealed to him something which had already existed deep within, waiting to be found.

It was with equal parts excitement and trepidation that he opened the plain brown package. Would it be as good as he'd remembered it? Admittedly, his memory was spotty. He couldn't remember exactly when or where he'd purchased the game, whether he'd received it as a gift or had bought it with his own money. He must have sold it along with all of his other youthful diversions after his enthusiasm for electronic gaming had given way to a thirst for outré books and music. Of all of the games he'd owned, he remembered this one the least. It seemed to exist as if through a veil, though it had certainly left its mark upon him.

After he had managed to track down a copy of the game and placed his order, Stefan immediately purchased a dusty old Atari 2600 Home Gaming Console at a local thrift store. In the event that the game actually arrived, he had every intention of playing it. The 2600 system was among the most primitive of the home gaming systems that had dominated the market in its time. Pixelated avatars traversed atrocious fields and castles; mazes made of blocky walls in a paltry variety of garish colors housed what passed for armored vehicles and deadly robots; candy-striped sunsets dominated bleak cityscapes in which poorly rendered atrocities unfolded with perplexing speed.

The action within the games was controlled by the player by means of a joystick with a single button.

For all of its unpleasantness, this particular gaming system was remembered both for its charm and for the ingenuity of its developers. It was a remarkably difficult system for which to program. The amount of memory available to each cartridge would scarcely constitute a joke in this day and age. In addition to that, the programmers were continually frustrated by the constraints of the cathode ray tube by which their games were to be displayed. An electron gun drew the contents of the screen, line by line, from left to right, from the top of the screen to the bottom. The stream of electrons was shot onto a bank of phosphates which lined the back of the glass comprising the television screen. By altering the position of the gun just a little, a different bank of phosphates would be activated, thus making it possible to produce a small variety of colors. It was only when the gun had finished a line and was automatically repositioned back to the left side of the screen to begin the next line that the computations needed to run the game could take place. All of this had to be meticulously timed. Failure to do so would result in catastrophic errors: an impossible field of shuddering glitches, the disappearance or random relocation of the player, a solid wall where there ought not to be one. Many of the early developers succumbed to a type of nervous exhaustion under which they were no longer able to do their jobs and were forced to take refuge in manual labor until their deranged minds were able to recover. What for many began as a dream job became an absolute nightmare.

Stefan never knew or cared about the perplexities of game development, however. His lot was to play, to immerse himself in the wondrous creations of these under-appreciated poets. Many were the games that he knew and loved between the ages of eight and thirteen, but none had so captured his imagination as the cartridge he now held, once again, in his very hands. He felt as if he'd recovered a long lost artifact belonging to an esoteric brotherhood of which he'd been a secret initiate.

His newly purchased prize came with no decorative box, no instruction booklet, not so much as a sticker on the front of the cartridge. The game came naked and austere, with nothing but the title embossed upon its upper surface: *A Book of Alabaster*. Stefan dimly remembered the instruction booklet that had come with the game he had owned in his youth, but he could not for the life of him remember what the box in which it came looked like, or the image which was displayed on the front of the cartridge. Many of the games released during the same era were indecipherable without the keys provided in their accompanying booklets. This would certainly have been the case with the game that he now held before him.

The gaming experience of *A Book of Alabaster* invariably began at the frog pond, and from there could proceed in any direction but back toward the bottom of the screen (there seemed to be a barrier of some sort which prevented downward or backward movement beyond the starting point). The principal locations to which Stefan's avatar had returned time and time again remained rooted in his memory like monoliths. Other details emerged, hazy and half-formed, occupying a region just beyond the veil of tangibility. A modicum of exploration, he vaguely recalled, revealed the chapel of sand, the deserted manor, and the salt mines. Hidden means of passage could be found beyond to other areas, or perhaps deeper into those ones. Somewhere in the salt mines had been found a phoenix made of lead, while the deserted manor concealed a sleeping quail somewhere in its depths—or was the quail located in a secret attic? The chapel of sand was frequented by a goat of benevolent disposition who walked upright on hind legs, though, as Stefan remembered it, the goat would only appear after certain areas had been uncovered, and during certain phases of the moon. Did the game have some kind of feature that indicated the passing of time? The details eluded him. Perhaps all of this had been explained in the instruction book.

Stefan had set up the gaming console with an old television set which sat upon a rustic Chinese bench. The arrangement was placed opposite a wall of bookshelves that obscured the floor to ceiling windows on one side of his tower apartment. Pushing the divan up against a perpendicular row of shelves which doubled as his bedroom wall allowed for the creation of a tiny space in which uninterrupted play could be enjoyed before a backdrop of the setting sun. Stefan sat himself before the console and inserted the cartridge into the game slot. The television screen flashed and stuttered as if choking on the dust of ancient stars. The momentary static flux gave way to a pinpoint of light, which extended into a horizontal line across the midpoint of the screen. The line extended all at once toward the upper and lower extremes of the display. Stefan felt his heart leap in nostalgic recognition as he gazed once again upon the pleasant vista of the frog pond.

The colors, just as he'd remembered them, were pleasingly muted in comparison to the more popular games of the time. The subtle hues found throughout the various regions of the game relaxed the eye. The pastoral effect produced thereby appeared open-ended and non-threatening. Stefan sat and stared for a while, delighted to revisit what had been a source of considerable fascination during his formative years. After several minutes had passed, he picked up one of the two joysticks which had come with the console and began to play.

He made his way gingerly up and to the left from his starting point, leaving the placid expanse of the frog pond behind him to explore the greater depths of the pixelated landscape. He plunged into a pleasant arrangement of hazy forests. Leafy treetops supported by boxy trunks rendered in a limited variety of browns and pale yellows flanked natural pathways leading off to unexplored horizons. Scattered clearings bejeweled with mossy boulders, barely recognizable as such, opened onto smaller ponds, impenetrable clumps of trees, rocky ledges. Stefan followed a river that wound through the trees, at length coming to a bridge over which he made his way to the other side.

Thus the hours passed, the sunset slowly giving way to evening and thenceforth into the perilous depths of night. It was just about the time at which the shadows had overcome the last remaining vestiges of day that Stefan became aware that the game which he was playing was not quite as he'd remembered it. He'd managed to find areas that in no way resembled the architecture of his cherished memories. There was a sort of barn, far off to the left beyond a wooded maze, which he felt quite certain that he was exploring for the first time. Intensive probing revealed a ladder concealed beneath an overhanging awning. A trap door was found as well, giving way to an area so dark that further headway was impossible for the time being. Could it be that Stefan had located a different version of the same game? He'd heard that variations had been introduced into international versions of some games by the manufacturer. Perhaps this was a later version than the one he'd owned, or an earlier one. It was just possible that he'd simply never found the barn when he was young, though this seemed exceedingly unlikely, as he was sure he'd spent an inordinate amount of time exploring its depths, leaving no stone unturned or pathway unexplored.

Stranger still, upon exploring an area far to the right of the place at which the game began, Stefan came across what looked to be an abandoned factory, its presence announced by scattered patches of weeds and rubble. Entrance into the factory was easily obtainable through any number of large holes left open in the decaying walls. Passage through the various sections of the factory proved much more difficult. The place was a perplexing maze of crumbling mortar and decrepit machinery.

This area was decidedly larger than any of the locations which Stefan remembered exploring in his youth. The factory encompassed at least four floors as well as an extensive basement, which itself hinted at the prospect of further depths below. The remaining hours of the night were spent exploring the dilapidated ruin. Stefan was powerless to tear himself away from it. At long last, just as the sun was beginning its treacherous climb back to the summit of the firmament, he was forced to break with his obsession and surrender to the tender embrace of sleep.

The office in which Stefan worked was as hermetic as his beloved lookout tower. He worked his own hours, which tended toward the later part of the day. The space in which he performed his daily duties was nothing if not intimate. It might have given rise to feelings of claustrophobia and confinement but for a couple of modest picture windows which looked out onto a backstreet graced with crumbling brick and ivy. Lack of sleep was not a problem in this place. His work was long familiar to him and required little effort. Stefan took his place before a bank of monitors and input devices and bumbled through an idle day translating technical requirements into blueprints. Dazed, not entirely present, he could think of nothing but his precious *Book of Alabaster*. It never once occurred to him to wonder what the name could possibly mean.

Back within the confines of the tower, he made a minimal effort to nourish himself before returning to the game. The urge to further penetrate its mysteries was almost overwhelming. Again he explored the untold depths of the factory building. Several new areas within the crumbling edifice were uncovered: a dimly lit office complex replete with locked doors and unserviceable elevators; a flooded display room crowded with wreckage; the entrance to a catacomb far beneath the level of the basement.

His excavations were occasionally intruded upon by a disturbing element of the game, an element that resembled nothing that he remembered encountering in his younger days. It seemed that he was not entirely alone in the abandoned factory. Every so often, perceptible only for a fleeting moment, Stefan caught sight of a dark personage darting from a shadow to a darkened doorway. It appeared to be a sort of gnome or dwarf. He never got the chance to examine it closely, though what brief glimpses he was afforded seemed to be rendered with startling malevolence. It is not easy for the 2600 system to support an image which carries an emotional resonance of any sort. Protagonists and antagonists alike are fleshed out with an appalling lack of detail. There seemed to be something about the dwarf, some combination of color and basic form, which struck a primal key. The thing made Stefan decidedly uneasy whenever it appeared.

Dinner was taken on the roof of the tower. No great affair; angel hair pasta with a smattering of sauce, a handful of oysters, a modicum of white wine to wash it down. He had to force himself to take the time required to prepare the meal. The effort was a mere formality, an act of willful restraint indulged in only to heighten the joy of reunion with his beloved. Within the space of thirty minutes he was again sitting before the television at the western window.

A few hours' further exploration revealed a new area on an upper floor of the factory. Access was gained to this level by way of a series of hidden service staircases and a maze of overturned desks. On one end of the building was found a clumsily rendered office complex of striking familiarity. Much of the area had been thoroughly explored before Stefan realized just to what degree the space bore an uncanny likeness to his own place of employment. Further still, in a remote corner of the complex, right at the place where it should naturally appear, was a small room not unlike the office in which he worked. Scarcely a moment after this had registered he noticed something else about the office which was in no uncertain terms alarming. Immediately behind a clumsy representation of a bank of monitors, before two picture windows, stood the malignant dwarf.

Stefan let out an audible yelp and dropped the joystick. The dwarf remained upon the screen, glaring at him with open contempt, until the reset switch was pressed. The frightful scene was swallowed in an ocean of black for just a fraction of a second before a shudder of static gave way to the reassuring vista of the frog pond.

Stefan sat in silence for some time, not sure what to do. Perhaps he'd been playing too much. Perhaps it might be wise to take a break. He could benefit from a decent amount of sleep for once (something of a rarity). He decided to take the next day off work. He thought it might be best as well to leave the game alone for the time being. He switched off the television set and went to bed.

Sleep was vexed by a series of perplexing dreams. One of them involved the game. The dream took place in a house in which Stefan had briefly lived with his mother when he was a child. The house had featured a lower-level basement apartment, occupied by an endless cycle of tenants and accessible through a separate door at the bottom of a concrete staircase. While he couldn't remember ever having actually seen the inside of the apartment, it occupied a crucial place in his imagination. It was as if it were a place forbidden to him, not by the dictates of the adults in his life, but by a sort of natural edict that he not enter therein.

In the dream, Stefan explored this area as if it were a part of the game. The underground apartment had expanded into a tremendous suite of rooms leading ever further downward beneath the surface of the earth. Everything was crystal clear, the concrete walls and tattered carpets were not pixilated or rendered in a limited color palette. Indeed, Stefan explored the area in person rather than through the medium of a television screen, yet the mood and character of the game were unmistakable. The finished basement gave way to a steam-filled tunnel. Stefan ventured further into the depths of the abysmal suite, spurred onward only by a perverse fascination. The presence of a variety of unfathomable inhabitants was felt, but never seen.

The following morning brought relaxation and repose. Eggs and sausage were enjoyed, mimosas were sipped, books were browsed. A hint of doubt accompanied the simple pleasures of the day. He could not quite piece together his youthful memories of *A Book of Alabaster* with other memories from the same time period. It was almost as if it had been somebody else that had played the game, and that person's reminiscence had somehow attached itself to his. He hadn't thought about the thing for ages before his recent surge of enthusiasm. It seemed odd that he would suddenly be so strongly drawn to it after all this time. He simply could not put this nagging doubt out of his head. He finally succumbed to the allure of the game just as the sun was announcing its descent.

Having decided to forgo further explorations of the factory for now, he pushed instead through a near impenetrable region beyond. Thick trees and crumbling walls of concrete proved an impediment to further navigation, expertly depicted through the limitations of the technology. With persistence, Stefan was able to find a way through to another area in the game: a series of interconnected caves which revealed themselves a little at a time. The cleverness of their construction, ingeniously making use of dark patches interspersed with light, both hampered and encouraged exploration. Scattered sections of what appeared to be the remains of a cathedral protruded from the depths from time to time, its decaying chapels and vestry providing both an aid and a hindrance to his progress. Fragments of stained glass occasionally emerged from natural crevices in the stone, the light streaming through the colorful tableaus playing out in dazzling displays upon the mossy undergrowth. At perilous moments, usually just as Stefan's avatar passed from one region of the subterranean tunnels to another, the whole earth seemed to shudder as if something of tremendous magnitude were taking place above the ground.

The need for sleep gradually overtook Stefan as the approach of morning threatened to swallow the night. He could not bear to lose the progress that he'd made thus far. Rather than turn the game off and start again the next day, he simply let it stand. It would be there for him when he awoke. By this point, it was a forgone conclusion that he would take another day off work.

Troublesome dreams again disturbed his slumber, this time far more vivid and strange. He found himself exploring a decrepit train yard filled with rusting hulks of metal. A stalking minotaur hauled chain-linked carriages of expired souls from the darkness of a tunnel which emerged from the bowels of the earth. Elsewhere, Stefan probed the depths of an underwater laboratory peopled by wooden horses of dark design. The painted bodies of the horses bore the icons of initiatory brotherhoods which stretched back through countless generations. Yet further, he visited an ancient and withered peacock in a parlor concealed in the hidden recesses of a plantation house. The peacock never spoke, yet it somehow managed to convey its murderous intention: an unspeakable plan involving a chess game played over the course of several centuries, resulting in multiple assassinations and betrayals.

Upon rising, Stefan plunged without hesitation back into the uncontrolled embrace of play. He occasionally allowed himself a brief respite for coffee or toast and jam, yet these digressions were kept short and to the point. With relish he returned to the object of his enthrallment.

It was well after the onset of night by the time he had finally managed to find his way through the twisty, winding tunnel system. What greeted him when he emerged from the dark, cramped labyrinth left him somewhat astounded. It was as if the earth had been scorched and tormented. Black fields filled with burnt and scattered bramble extended endlessly in every direction. The fact that the ruined environment was rendered through such a primitive lens made it appear all the more destitute. Nothing further stood in his path. He found that he could wander for an extended period of time in any direction and encounter little but scant variations on the same patterns of patchy weed and charred ground. He resolved to venture upward in the direction of the top of the screen (the player icon remained ever in the center). This he did as the hours passed. He felt little regret for the time forever lost to what appeared to be a fruitless venture into nothing.

After a seemingly endless stretch of time, and long after the veil of night had fallen, Stefan came across something different than anything he'd seen before. The sight which he encountered at the edge of the wrecked and ravaged land left him absolutely certain that he had never played this game when he was young. What was taking place was beyond his understanding. He'd long been ignoring the obvious fact that it would not be possible for any game made for this particular system to give way to such a rich and varied playing experience. The amount of memory allotted to the 2600 cartridge was truly pitiable. Both the experience that he was having, and the memory of the game that had seemed to be his own, were impossible. He was compelled to accept the truth of the matter. The terrifying absurdity of his situation could no longer be denied.

He would seem to have encountered an angel of sorts. A fiery behemoth of unbearable proportions, covering an area far larger than the screen could depict at any one time. Whether it was truly a malevolent entity or simply too outlandish for his mind to grasp, it was a horrific sight. A continual flow of chills ran down Stefan's spine, yet still he could not tear himself away from the screen. He wandered in a daze through the landscape of its body as a cacophony of flames and wings fluctuated around him, all bespotted with eyes arranged in perplexing patterns that opened and closed in apparently random succession. One thing was certain, if a single individual had been responsible for this monstrous creation, that person was an absolute genius. Of course, Stefan knew that this could not have been the case.

The being, celestial or infernal, seemed to be wholly immaterial, insomuch as Stefan's avatar could pass right through its body. Though it made him terrifically uncomfortable, he plodded onward, advancing ever further into the kingdom of malaise. Sodom and Gomorrah, Babylon and Edom, every cursed city of which it has been written seemed to rise and fall within that pulsating mass of feather and flame. The holy of holies in the heavenly Jerusalem and the hallowed halls of Tartarus beneath the mantle of the earth were reflected in equal measure in the penetrating eyes of the bewildering beast. Yet Stefan persisted, determined to see the ordeal through to the very end.

At last, the terrible vision of the angel seemed to part, leaving Stefan in a truly empty place. No longer did the soil appear to be tortured, for there was no soil at all, nor brick nor stone nor shattered tree nor bramble; nothing but a smooth expanse of quiet gray inclined to black. Onward, ever onward through the night of desolation did Stefan proceed, scarcely any longer aware of his own body.

Time seemed to cease. Direction of travel lost all relevance. There was no place to go, and yet the journey continued. Countless hours passed without a hint of variation. Not a single trace of sanctuary lay anywhere in sight. Would there be no end?

And yet an end did come. After an indeterminate time of compulsive play with no reward, a boundary etched in white descended from the upper edge of the screen. As the approaching structure came increasingly into view it took on the shape and definition of a house. By the time the front door had nearly come to meet the middle of the screen its significance was clear. The likeness of the lookout tower had been rendered in surprising detail. Stefan ascended the staircase along one side, passing through the open door that let into the base of the tower. A short trip up the winding stairs and into the tower's summit revealed the apartment exactly as it was, not omitting Stefan's lifeless shell before the console at the western window. The television screen, as rendered within the game, was filled with a solid, pulsing light, as if it were the breath of dying suns forgotten in the emptiness of space. The light gradually came to dominate the screen, revealing faint hints of writing on its surface, characters from some lost alphabet traced into the luminous essence. This must be it! The Book of Alabaster! Treasure of treasures, long sought after but impossible to possess! All the seekers in the world couldn't find it, and those that found it would never be able to contain it. Yet here it was, falling away. The book grew smaller and smaller until all that remained was a single pixel, flashing and scintillating like a spark of immaculate perfection in the endless night.

The Music of Exile

The Poetess

SNOWFLAKES fell from the naked sky in silent droves. They alighted on the surface of Karina's cigarette and suffused the tobacco inside with their icy and impartial touch. She followed the familiar detour from the main road, her path marked out by the boot prints of another who'd arrived before her. The last rays of the dying sun had nearly been extinguished. The shadows had come marching in like foot soldiers, overthrowing the reign of twilight and concealing the winter landscape beneath an intoxicating shroud of sapphire.

Karina made her way down the precarious decline before the scrutiny of a court of snow-covered alders. So far as she knew, the trees continued on for several miles. She placed the cigarette between her lips and partook of its luxuriant flavor as her destination came into view. This would mark the third time that she had visited the Stenger house in as many years. It shone like an effulgent lantern at the bottom of the hill, the expansive windows emanating a lush, orange glow.

She managed, with a little effort, to make it to the front porch without slipping, flicking the remains of her cigarette into the snowy wastes before sounding the doorbell. The chateau did not appear to be particularly ostentatious from the outside. It was sizable, yet modest in design. The inside, on the other hand, was like a reliquary, harboring mysteries of décor that seemed to seep into her dreams on those occasions on which she slept beneath its roof.

After a moment's wait, the door opened wide on its hinges, revealing Konrad in his usual impeccable attire. "Karina, my indomitable poetess, your presence comes as a great relief," he said, ushering her into the foyer. "Come in! You must be freezing. Your name was just on our lips when we heard the bell."

"I hope I haven't kept you waiting," said Karina as she crossed over the threshold and into the house of patronage. "Would you believe I missed my train?"

"In this house, we'll believe absolutely anything," said Konrad. "Your coat, your scarf, your notable lack of gloves or hat," he prompted, "simply hand them over to me and I will dispose of them for you. You are alarmingly underdressed for this unfortunate weather."

"As a would-be poet, I claim to be impervious to the elements." Karina slipped out of her winter garments with the elegance of a chanteuse.

"Neither Urban nor Katja will be here with us tonight," lamented Konrad as he shuttled the heavy coat and scarf into the foyer closet. "As it turns out, they didn't even make it to the station before turning back. But come in, come in! I'll have soup for you in a few minutes."

Karina remained alone in the foyer for just a moment after Konrad had made his exit into the spacious main room. The chateau had thus far never failed to exert a dazzling effect upon her senses. A carpet of crimson and bright saffron continued up the center of a narrow stairway opposite the door. Brass statues of women clad in flowing robes stood on the lower extremes of the handrails. An arm was raised above each of their heads, their upturned palms supporting spherical bulbs of soft, yellow light. Though their faces were dispassionate beneath the radiance of the lamps, a subtle hint of defiance could be discerned in their expressions. They seemed, between themselves, to harbor an inclination toward sedition and dissent. Some distance above them, beyond the summit of the stairs, an arch of stained glass suffused the upper landing in soft shades of azure and vermilion.

Opposite the main room resided Lena's studio. A curtain drawn across the doorway concealed its interior from sight. Niches opened in the walls next to the doors on either side of the foyer. These were occupied by wonders of taxidermy fashioned by the mistress of the house herself. A Japanese thrush guarded the entrance to the studio, its open beak inclined upward as if to ward off intruders. A tiny wound opened in its speckled breast from which emerged a third claw, toes splayed wide and fraught with urgency. The impression was that of a second bird escaping from the interior of the first. In the opposing niche, a vivid green parrot from Sri Lanka perched upon a wooden stand, its eyes inset with shining rubies beneath the rush of scarlet which crowned its head. Karina fished a cigarette from the opened package inside of her handbag. This she placed upon the ledge before the jeweled bird as she strode past its niche and into the brightly lit space beyond.

The main room of the Stenger house was an orgy of plaster, white marble, stained wood and gold trim. Two pillars that rose from floor to ceiling separated one end of the room from the other. An enormous polished wooden table dominated the far end, while the nearer half was arranged in the style of an open study. Bookshelves stocked with scandalous titles framed a pleasing arrangement of slender couches and divans. A writing desk kept company with an apothecary cabinet. Statuettes and *objets d'art* luxuriated in the radiance of a painting of a woman in flaming vermillion traversing a corridor of petrified wood.

Lena sat at one end of the dining table, glass of chilled Chablis in hand. She looked as elegant as ever beneath the soft glow of the chandelier, with her fiery auburn hair and long grey dress. The only other guest that would be present that evening was seated on one of two quaint armchairs before the windows in the far corner. Karina had been steeling herself for their meeting from the moment she'd left her apartment. The woman had short blonde hair, supple like goose-down, and skin as smooth as lustrous ivory. She looked like a czarina with her artless face and dark, compelling eyes. Her jaw was fit for ancient statuary, noble and tenacious. A pendant of polished onyx stood out against her white button-up top. She reclined in her chair with her hands gently folded in her lap, an untouched glass of wine on a small table beside her.

"There you are, my dove," said Lena, rising from her chair. "I have long looked forward to this meeting. Karina Takala," she let an elegant hand fall in the direction of the woman in the armchair, "Anna Reznikova."

Anna rose with the finesse of an ibis and cast an admiring glance upon her fellow poet. Karina simply stood and clutched her handbag before her. The woman was much taller than she'd expected her to be. She gave a slight bow of the head, hoping to conceal her trepidation beneath a veil of courtesy. "It's an honor to meet you," she said. "I must confess, I am somewhat of an enthusiast in regards to your work."

"An odious confession, indeed," returned Anna, with an affable gaze. She extended a slender hand, which Karina took into her own. "I hear you are a poet as well," she said. "That's two black marks against you. You are well on your way to a fabulous infamy."

Karina had managed to track down a handful of lengthy selections of verse that the Russian poet had published over the years. These were printed, without exception, in limited edition journals, some of which had proven nearly impossible to obtain. Anna was anything but well known, yet the ardent devotion of her admirers was noteworthy. Her work had never been collected, and she seemed to prefer it that way. Obscurity suited her. It could almost be said to be an aspect of her art.

"I was just bragging about your poetry, in fact," said Lena, as she poured a glass of wine for her guest. "Your work has a playful quality about it that is quite unlike anything I've seen elsewhere. I've been looking forward all week to hearing excerpts from your latest efforts."

"Your flattery pleases and baffles me in equal measure," said Karina, seating herself at the far end of the table as if to shield herself from the overwhelming presence of the two women. "To be quite honest, I'm not entirely convinced that I've yet found my voice."

"A poet can never be said entirely to find her voice," said Anna, her eyes bathed in pools of dark blue shadow. "Poetry is the music of exile. It defines itself not by revealing, but by concealing. The best poets are perfectly invisible, as anonymous as the night itself."

Karina was surprised to detect a subtle element of drollery that attended Anna's every word and gesture. She spoke with no trace of an accent. It was clear from her speech, as with her poetry, that she had thoroughly mastered a language which was not her own. Her statements almost seemed to ridicule themselves, so light and insouciant was their delivery. This quality stood in perfect opposition to the tone of her work, which was unfailingly solemn and momentous.

Konrad reappeared a moment later carrying a wide bowl of lobster bisque that had been garnished with a perfectly symmetrical arrangement of finely chopped chives. Once the dish was served and adequately peppered, he sat himself beside the Russian poet and launched into an exposition on the relative merits of chance and determination in the creative process. His own opinion, he was not shy to proclaim, was that chance operations were indispensable. The artist, he insisted, must sell their soul to something larger than their ego, and which they can never truly hope to understand. What they received in return for the transaction, if their soul was not found wanting, was the raw material for new creation. Lena maintained that a true artist would never condescend to sell their soul. They would prefer, rather, to misplace it or to gamble it away, ever cognizant of the poetic virtue that attends the heedless act.

"The soul of the artist is like poison," remarked Anna. "Selling it is hardly a viable option. The devil himself will have nothing to do with it."

"Our good Doctor Faust would seem to have proven otherwise," said Konrad.

"Faustus was a scholar, not an artist," replied Anna. "The former observes the sanctum of truth from the safety of its outer court, while the latter brazenly strides in and defiles the altar."

Karina sipped her wine in silence, enjoying the easy pleasure that came with passively participating in a compelling conversation. She wondered what Anna would have to say in regards to the *Faustus* of Thomas Mann, but she kept her tongue restrained. Konrad rose to shuttle her empty soup bowl back to the kitchen, refilling her wine glass upon his return. Having seated himself once more, he politely requested that Karina regale them with excerpts from her latest work.

Karina took a petite black notebook from her handbag, every page of which was crowded with handwriting so tiny as to be unreadable to any but herself. "I have, in fact, prepared some passages for this evening," she said, as she opened the book before her. "Though I feel I must give fair warning. My offerings are taken from a work in progress which I fear is turning out to be somewhat of a whimsical piece."

"Duly noted," affirmed Konrad from his armchair, his chin slightly upraised as he held his glass before him.

Karina flipped through the pages of her notebook, suddenly not entirely certain which of several fragments she'd prefer to start with. The prospect of exposing her most intimate reflections before Anna made her nervous in the extreme. On her previous visits, she'd delivered recitals before novelists, musicians, painters, and even journalists. Never before had she shared her work with a fellow poet, much less one that she so ardently admired. Both Konrad and Lena had always showered her with praise, and she'd received fairly good reviews in the few journals that had agreed to print her work. And yet it seemed to her that poets shared a complex protocol between them, a set of rites and strictures that lay beyond her comprehension but which she was bound to all the same. The thought of engaging with these unspoken customs at once terrified and fascinated her. Even the most unintentional of violations, she felt, would incur undesirable consequences.

At last, she settled on a place to start. She took a sip of wine, let the crisp minerality of the golden nectar provoke her palate, and commenced her reading, endeavoring to properly enunciate the underlying rhythm of the piece despite her agitation. She cast her eyes up at her audience for a single moment before lowering them again to the pages of the book.

> "Ill at ease in the embrace of night," she began,
> "I slip out of the sleeping house, take flight.
> I flee like an apostate beneath the fiery stars
> Of winter, a stale cigarette in my hand
> And a match with which to forge my name.
> The night guard at the border
> Stamps my passport with the flame;
> It glistens like a stain.
> Sentinels, like threads of golden bells,
> Mouth holds taste of night-spells.
> I lose myself beneath the pale sublime,
> The stars that weep secrete strange wine."

Here she gave the slightest pause, long-practiced, before continuing, the tempo of her delivery increasing by an almost imperceptible degree.

> "I come across a penitentiary
> That hides beneath the wind,
> The prisoners must enter from behind.

From a window, high above
Falls the shadow of the commandant,
A flock of bureaucrats behind him
Holding tall white candles
and announcing edicts.
They issue statements,
Signed and notified,
To a machine which mutters
in its sleep.
Its revelations are distributed
To the prisoners
And their savants.
Mystified, I strain to comprehend
The mysteries which to my ears descend
As I crouch below the window, pale with fright,
Ill at ease in the embrace of night."

Karina desperately wished that she had a cigarette in her free hand. She'd watched some of the other guests smoke without hindrance inside of the house, yet had never quite felt confident enough to do so herself. She let the final lines of the second verse hang frozen in the air for a few seconds before she continued with her arduous exposition.

"My vision is a flaming candlestick,
Conspiracies of light consume the wick,
The wax is swallowed by the stratosphere,
The candle-holder disappears.
The flame alone remains, its golden radiance
Consumes me. I find myself inside a house
Containing not a single room.

The prison guards have all escaped,
They've slipped out through the iron gate,
I tremble like a thief, a cornered field mouse, a leaf.
I yearn to snuff my candle and take flight,
Ill at ease within the light."

Again she stole a glance at her audience, startled just a little at the attention that Anna, in particular, lavished upon her from her chair by the windows. The ghost of a wry smile appeared upon the elder poet's face. The woman seemed to look right into her, fixing her attention on something that Karina was not familiar with herself. She turned her attention back to the open page before her, relieved that the reading was nearly through.

"This repository stands without a door," she read,
"Nor walls or windows, ceiling or a floor.
A sea of geese, a flock of migrant doves,
A music box, a pair of silken gloves,
A jeweled quail, a riot of cormorants,
A peacock traced in rust and lighting,
A nightingale flown deep inside a well,
A canticle condemned to hell,
I catalog these relics with delight,
Ill at ease in the embrace of night."

Karina placed the book down before her, cover closed, a sheepish glance turned up toward her peers as if awaiting a pronouncement of their judgment. A round of applause was cheerfully bestowed upon her. She was especially pleased to see Anna placing her hands together in a gesture of seeming sincerity. "I'll read more later, if you want it," she said. "I don't think I can manage more than a little at a time."

"Poetry loses its potency if taken in too large a measure," said Anna, the chandelier above casting a hypnotic arrangement of light and shadow across the contours of her face. "I am pleased with your work."

Karina flushed with modesty. The compliment seemed all the more heartfelt for its understated simplicity. It may have been the only straightforward remark that Anna had produced all evening.

Another round of wine was poured, necessitating the opening of a second bottle. Konrad applied himself to the task with mathematical precision. A complex methodology was employed, entirely opaque to all but himself, to ensure that the two wines were properly distributed among the guests. Conversation resumed, giving way a meandering drift in which several topics and themes were mirrored and transposed as in a musical score. Karina, relieved at having survived her first ordeal of the evening, simply let herself relax, quietly taking in the splendors of décor with which the main room was nearly overwhelmed. Just above her, upon the white marble surface of a wooden cabinet, perched an arctic owl whose silky breast was hung with a variety of antiquated war medals. Its imperious brown eyes gazed out over the table with a look of urgency. The beast resembled a retired general who had just disclosed a piece of classified intelligence which invalidated a long established truth.

After several lines of inquiry had been elucidated, it was decided that the time had come for Anna's reading. Her single offering for the evening was a fairly lengthy composition involving an excommunicated prioress possessed of an insatiable thirst for the unfathomable. The piece began with an immaculate description of a long and tenuous crossing by water. The faith of the holy woman flamed like a torch in the night sea air, illuminating the encroaching darkness as the rising waves threatened to overturn her tiny boat. She prayed, throughout the course of several memorable stanzas, to be reduced to nothing but the ardor of her aspiration. This she fervently desired so that she might come at last, having relinquished all else, to gain an intimate knowledge of the mind of her creator.

Karina was at once overpowered by the potency of the piece and humbled by its eloquence, yet she couldn't help but think again of Doctor Faustus. The woman in the poem would seem to seek a covenant with God, reducing her own essence that a greater understanding might be bestowed upon her. The arrangement seemed to mirror the tradition of the learned doctor entering into a contract with the devil. She thought of the notorious arts of the Kabbalists, employing complex permutations of the names of the Divine in order to attain to hidden knowledge. She felt that all of these narratives were little more than variations on a single theme. Karina knew that she would not be able to read another selection of her own work that night. Her efforts would be dwarfed by Anna's.

"I have not a single religious bone in my entire body," said Lena, her chin resting on one hand, "yet the beauty of your work can almost make me understand the faith and motivations of the ascetic."

"Where a scholar clothes the truth in falsehood," observed Anna, "the lies of a poet attempt to reveal the truth in all of its nakedness. I won't deny that mine is a deceitful art."

"Let us not forget," insisted Konrad, "that the artist and the academic are quite dependent upon one another."

"We are inseparably bound, it's true," said Anna, her dark eyes sparkling with furtive levity. "We're beholden to ancient pacts forged by our most distant ancestors."

Cardamom cake was served with coffee. An ornate candelabra was systematically illuminated as the chandeliers were doused. The flames danced in entrancing rhythms across the imposing artwork that adorned the walls, the bookshelves and the objects that inhabited them, and the polished wooden surface of the table. Lena fetched a cello from her studio and treated the guests to a few related fragments of her most recent work in progress. Karina let the music wash over her like a complex combination of fragrances as she sipped her coffee. Lena's composition was every bit as haunting and compelling as was her taxidermy. Karina felt as though she were a trespasser in the company of genius. Even Konrad, with his years' worth of research, lectures, and published studies, towered above her in experience and acumen.

The evening officially drew to a close after Lena's presentation was completed. "Come the morning," announced Konrad, "we'll serve crêpes and caviar, champagne and bourbon, coffee with holy oil, or whatever else you might desire; perhaps Karina will be so kind as to ennoble our spirits with another reading." The two poetesses, the younger and the elder, were shown up to their bedrooms for the night. Anna was to sleep on a fold-out bed in Konrad's office, while Karina was given the guest bedroom proper. She was almost glad that Urban and his wife had been unable to make it. During previous visits to the Stenger house, it had been necessary for her to share a room with another guest. Sleeping in the same space as Anna, she feared, would be too much for her. She imagined lying awake throughout the night, overstimulated by the near presence of the superior poet. In any case, she preferred to have a room in the house entirely to herself. The character and subtleties of both the upstairs office and the guest room had long appealed to her aesthetic sensibilities.

The Passport

Karina was an incorrigible traveler. She never took a single thing with her, save her modest handbag. Cigarettes and matches, house key and black notebook, a miniature volume of Mallarmé, some bank notes, and identification were all she felt she ever needed. She was more than happy to sleep in her clothes. She rarely wore makeup, and made a point of going bare-faced when she stayed with others. If she couldn't go a single night without a toothbrush, so she thought, then she could hardly call herself a poet. She derived a particular pleasure from travelling light.

The guest bedroom could well have been a second office. A heavy writing desk faced the wall opposite the bed, while two doorways that opened into a dark walkthrough closet beckoned from its either side. A small cabinet of rough-grained wood clung to the wall atop the desk, flanked by shapely wall-mounted lamps that bathed the room in a perplexing network of crisscrossing shadows. Atop the surface of the cabinet perched another of Lena's creations; an Australian raven, black as pitch, with wings tucked in a studious manner behind its back. A circle of yellow eyes peered out from beneath the feathers on its breast, in addition to the two that resided where they ought to be, above the beak. Karina had seen the piece before. It reminded her of a professor. It seemed intent on maintaining a careful scrutiny of the occupant of the room as they slept.

At the head of the bed, above a rich mahogany headboard replete with ornamental fretwork, hung a framed illustration bathed in shadow. The image depicted a scorpion, its pincers reaching toward the bottom of the frame while the stinger was raised in a treacherous arc near the top. It appeared to traverse the surface of a cluttered workspace. A fragment of a compass could be seen to one side, along with a straightedge and graphite pencil. The body of the predator itself obscured a portion of a city map. As Karina sat on one edge of the bed and contemplated the meticulous line work with which the image had been drawn, she was struck by a resemblance, in temperament if not physique, to the poet in the room next to her own. She didn't think that Anna was in any way malicious—in fact she came across as rather benign—yet there seemed always to be a drop of poison concealed in her recondite wit.

The remainder of the décor was fairly unremarkable. Low bookshelves crammed with academic texts stood to either side of the bed, one of them supporting a decorative lamp to allow for nighttime reading. Two sizable windows looked out onto a desolate expanse of snow, the white earth mirrored by a bed of luminous cloud that spread itself across the heavens.

There was something in Karina's temperament that would not allow her to sleep, whether as a guest or in her own apartment, before a sufficiently advanced hour had come to pass. It was customary for her, when she stayed at the Stenger house, to spend the first half of the night reclining on one of the couches downstairs, a book in hand and the diffuse glow of one of the tall standing lamps shed over her. She would be afforded little more than a few hours' sleep, but this hardly bothered her. The ground-floor library was more than sufficient to keep her amused until exhaustion finally arrived. On previous visits, she'd immersed herself in such curiosities as a slender volume of pornographic verse involving intricate machines and wooden dolls, a compendium of cartographical conspiracies that had perpetuated themselves throughout the ages, a catalog of gnostic heresies penned by an eighteenth-century civil servant, and a lengthy paean to the noble bureaucrat, along with several other tantalizing volumes. Looking forward to several hours of solitude in a place with which she was only passably familiar, and to the rich array of treasures that she'd inevitably unearth, she headed down the stairs and passed once more between the disconsolate couple who presided over the threshold of the lower floor.

Before perusing the bookshelves, Karina spent some time examining a board game which resided on a cabinet shelf behind glass doors near one of the windows. The design had been hand-painted directly onto a thick square of dark wood. One end of the board was inset with a silver handle between a pair of latches which had been affixed with tiny screws. The squares of a grid, consisting of thirteen rows of thirteen columns, were decorated each with a pair of letters painted side by side, black on silver alternating with white on black. The pieces, which were distributed unevenly among the squares as if a game was currently in progress, consisted of small wooden pyramids with their faces painted in a variety of lively colors. These were decorated with characters that resembled mathematical symbols or figures found in alchemical texts. The game appeared to be so complex as to be unreasonable to play.

The light touch of footsteps and the muffled creak of shifting wood could be heard from the foyer behind her. She turned around to find Anna passing like a holy dove beneath the shadow of the archway. The Russian poetess, taking note of the assemblage that had attracted Karina's scrutiny, proceeded to elucidate the history of the piece with every measure of her usual eloquence. "It was created by a book binder from New Jersey," she said, seating herself upon the divan next to the cabinet, "a recluse and a misanthrope, according to most accounts. The artwork is part of a limited edition, each created by hand and designed with subtle variations in the layout of the squares and pieces. He's gone so far as to publish a compendium of rules for play," she claimed, "a technical monstrosity of over one thousand pages which is full of contradictions and logical impossibilities. It reads, in some parts, like a political manifesto, in others like a dream journal. It even contains a script for an operetta."

Given the absence of the book in question and the playful demeanor with which it was described, Karina was fairly confident that Anna had invented it on the spot. She looked so comfortable with herself as she reclined against the sloping back of the divan. Karina clasped her hands before her and cast her eyes toward the shelves as if in search of a particular title.

"Your work made an impression upon me," said Anna, her fingers gently interlaced upon the immaculate folds of her skirt.

"I'm more than a little flattered," said Karina as she turned her eyes toward her unlikely admirer. "I'm relieved that my reading came off alright, actually. I find it difficult to read my own work."

"Were I inclined to lie, I would assure you that it grows easier with time," remarked Anna. "To this day, I hate to read my poetry aloud. With a little practice, you'll learn to hide your disdain for the task every bit as effectively as I do."

"I've been warned that the feeling of being an imposter never entirely goes away," said Karina. "When I present my work, I feel as though I'm exposing something I ought not to be, as if I'd crossed a line and shed a light on something that would prefer to remain unseen."

"It's a natural feeling," said Anna, her voice edged with a hint of irony. "Poetry and trespass are synonymous. Every good poetic work involves a crucial act of theft. It is part of the nature of our fire that it must be stolen."

Karina blessed Anna's statement with her tacit approval. She harbored a growing desire to break the cryptic aphorisms that the poet dispensed into pieces that she might carefully scrutinize their constituent elements. They were never wholly serious, yet each of them seemed to illuminate a precept at once familiar and perplexing. It was as if she held a mirror before her as she conversed, but the angle at which she held it caused the reflection to distort in a manner that dazzled the viewer.

"It's often said that a person cannot become a poet," said Anna, "but that a poet must be born so. I'm happy to inform you that this is entirely a myth, or at best a half-truth. There is a method by which the tenuous connection to the muse may be solidified, and thus the volatile be made fixed."

Karina was perfectly flummoxed. She had every desire to respond to Anna's assertion, but not a single word with which to do so.

"The process is not without complexity," the woman continued. "The key lies in a formula concealed within the works of the most notorious of our predecessors. It is not a matter in which I lack experience." Anna extended one arm over the upper ridge of the divan, fingers gently curling over the wooden crest. Her countenance was a mystery to poets and priests alike. "There exists every possibility, if you are so inclined, that we could undergo the operation tonight," she continued. "I believe I have the necessary means."

Karina responded with dignity and self-possession, allowing herself to enter into the spirit of Anna's whimsy. "I will gladly undergo whatever trials you wish to put before me," she said, head slightly bowed and hands still clasped before her.

"You should know that the process isn't foolproof," warned Anna, as she sat up on the edge of the divan. "It must be carried out in two parts. From time to time, the first phase doesn't take and the undertaking must be abandoned. There is an element of risk as well. The operation has been known, on occasion, to incur unintended liabilities."

"I'm willing to accept the risk," affirmed Karina, speaking on little more than bluster and blind faith.

"I had a feeling that it was so," said Anna as she rose from the divan, the dim light of the reading lamps cascading like water over her elegant attire. "Let us retire to the upstairs office. The setting is more studious than I'd prefer, but it should prove adequate enough for our purposes. At the very least, I don't think we'll be lacking in supplies."

With that she headed back toward the foyer. Karina dutifully followed her beneath the adjoining arch. She had not the slightest clue as to Anna's intentions, yet she was inclined to oblige the elder poet. Delphic and oblique she most certainly was, but she hardly seemed untrustworthy. The possibility that her elaborate game concealed an eccentric attempt at seduction had crossed her mind, but her intuition told her that this was not so. The woman exuded a sense of benevolence as if it were a rare perfume.

Anna passed like an exquisite ghost between the statues at the base of the stairs, her step restrained by an economy of movement that perfectly reflected the precision of her art. Karina followed after her with a noticeably coarser and less worldly gait. She couldn't shake the feeling that the robed women that rose from the bannisters were somehow complicit with the Russian poet. The glowing bulbs they raised above their heads were now the single source of light to the foyer, the overhead lamp having been switched off when the hosts retired for the night. The shadows had shifted in their positions on their faces as a result of the change in lighting. They no longer appeared quite so contentious as they had before. They looked, rather, like saints engaged in the silent adoration of an unknowable god.

The upstairs office was chiefly occupied with a long wooden desk before two spacious windows, its surface organized with an inexplicable symmetry that revealed Konrad's obsessive hand. Bookshelves lined the majority of the open wall space, while the far end of the room was given entirely to a pair of elegant glass doors. The space beyond, now thoroughly covered in snow, comprised little more than a platform surrounded by a low balustrade. Precisely in the center of the room, without the luxury of a supporting wall, lay a fold-out bed fitted with ebony blankets and pillows encased in crimson silk. Karina had slept in the exact same bed two times before. It looked perfectly incongruous in the academic atmosphere of the office.

Within seconds, the bed had been stripped of blankets, folded up, and pushed back against a row of shelves. Anna opened up her modest travel bag and removed an item wrapped in fine white linen. This she handed to her novitiate, who stood with affected nonchalance before the glass doors at the far end of the room. "Unwrap them," she instructed. "You'll want to become as familiar with them as possible over the next few minutes. Touch them, smell them, let their aesthetic permeate your senses. Try to discern the subtle essence that courses through them like the blood of the savior in a consecrated host."

Upon removing the inner contents from their wrapping, Karina found a deck of playing cards that seemed to have been culled from several vastly different sets. While many of them were either of poker or bridge size, enough were slightly off in either magnitude or proportion to make them awkward to handle. They were far less than fifty-two in number. Not a single court card could be found among them. Their faces were adorned with magpies and parakeets, owls and ostriches, ibises, wrens, and several other types of bird, all artfully positioned around the familiar hearts, diamonds, clubs, and spades, which were arranged in the expected patterns according to their value. Karina imagined that Anna had painstakingly collected them, one at a time, most likely over a long period. As far as she could ascertain, no two cards in the deck were of the same design.

Karina held the cards before her mouth and nostrils, allowing their subtle perfume to suffuse her. They were not strongly scented, yet they did exude a particular mix of essences: vanilla wrapped in a haze of musk and spiked with a hint of sweet tobacco. The scent seemed to link them to their owner, though she couldn't say exactly how. Their individual odors must have gradually mingled throughout the time that they'd been gathered together.

Looking up from her examination, she found Anna casting her eyes about the room as if in search of something. Two items lay at her feet, both of which Karina recognized as having been taken from the many curiosities distributed about the office. The first was a Chinese match safe made of silver, its surface engraved with an erotic image of a nude woman standing on one leg upon a precipice and blowing through a long wooden horn. The other was a single cubical die of hand-carved wood. The six faces were unpainted, while the shallow depressions carved upon them had been carefully stained with ink. Anna's eye seized on a metronome which rested atop one of the bookcases. The case was carved from rosewood, and the brass fittings shone with a dull luster beneath the overhead light. This she retrieved and placed upon the floor next to the other items.

"I think we have what we need," she said, holding out one hand as she turned her attention to the younger poet.

Karina passed the cards back with their wrapping gently folded underneath. She watched with curiosity as Anna carefully cycled through them. She repeatedly shifted the topmost card to the bottom until, with a determination and resolve born of long experience, she selected one among them and held it in the air before her. After taking a moment to consider her choice, she stepped before the work desk and let the chosen card fall from between her fingers. It sank like a stone, landing on one corner on the polished floorboards before it fell face-down, the design upon the back just visible in the dim light. She repeated the process several times, slowly tracing an ill-defined circle of cards around the open space. Some fell with their faces turned upward, some with their faces concealed. She remained positively sphinx-like as she proceeded, the funereal demeanor she had assumed during her reading enveloping her like an impregnable fortress.

Karina stood with fingers interlaced before her as her newfound mentor prepared the space. She allowed her gaze to meander about the room as the woman retrieved several short white candles from her travel bag and meticulously began to place them on the surfaces of the cards. In the space between the windows above the writing desk hung a counterpart to the illustration in the adjoining room. A swan rose above a cubic block of wood, its majestic wings outstretched toward the upper limits of the frame. The cube was engraved with letters from the Roman alphabet in various fonts and sizes. Some were reversed while others were inverted; all of them arranged upon the three visible faces of the cube to no discernable purpose. As with the scorpion, the graceful beast seemed to demonstrate a significant facet of Anna's nature. The two sides were as dependent upon each other as were the aesthete and the intellectual. Karina wondered at her tendency to see the qualities of the Russian poet in both of the portraits. There must be something to the woman's character, she mused, that tended to reflect itself in the elements of her environment.

"The difference between a poet and a charlatan," said Anna, once all thirteen candles had been set in place, "is that the former improvises, whereas the latter merely makes things up." She stood within the circle on the side closest to the work desk, the silken folds of her pale skirt nearly touching the floor above her soft leather boots. "I think we're ready to begin," she said.

A wide grin formed upon Karina's face, revealing a row of slightly crooked teeth. Anna instructed her to sit within the circle so that they faced one another from opposing sides. The match safe and the die had been placed between them, along with a long white taper and a box of matches. "The candles must be lit in order," instructed the elder poet, "beginning with the one directly behind me and advancing clockwise. You must imagine that the flame is being transferred from card to card, like the repetition of verse from mouth to ear. Thus do we perpetuate the heresies that flamed upon the altars of our predecessors." She lit the taper with a match before handing it to Karina, who carried out her task exactly as instructed. When she was finished, Anna snuffed the candle flame between two fingers.

The rite that followed required each of them to take one of the two items that lay between them into their left hands. Anna chose the match safe, leaving the other to take up the die. "Wood and silver harbor sympathies and antipathies which are invaluable to workings of this type," she explained. "Now, place your right hand in mine." Upon making contact, Karina was surprised to sense a tangible flow of force between them. It felt as if a magnetic current passed directly from Anna's hand to hers, making itself known in the form of a slight pulse between their palms. In addition, a subtle tension was perceptible between the match safe and the wooden die. These sensations evoked a sense of intimacy with the other woman that lay just beyond Karina's comfort range.

"I assume you can recite your work from memory?" confirmed Anna. The younger poet merely nodded.

"Good," she said. "It will be necessary for us to mingle the streams between us."

The front panel of the metronome was unlatched and removed, the key wound up, and the pendulum adjusted to keep time at fifty-two ticks per minute. With a quick pass of the hand, the machine was set in motion. Eye contact was initiated, with the unspoken understanding that it not be broken. Anna began with a line from the poem that she'd read earlier in the evening. Karina followed, a little uncertain as to whether her contribution was recited exactly as it was written in her notebook. She was distracted by the ticking of the metronome. Its rhythm interfered with the meter of her recitation, providing a notable strain against which she was forced to exert an effort. As the exercise continued, line by line, she became increasingly aware of an ascending dignity which attended Anna's speech. The grandeur of her delivery, soft-spoken as it was, seemed to overwhelm the contending cadence of the mechanical device. This was effected both through the haunting beauty of her imagery and by way of a sinuous flame that seemed to reside within her very words. Karina got the definite impression that she was intended to emulate the older woman.

With each line, the younger poet attempted to take up the thread laid down for her, yet by the time she'd reached the final syllable it had again managed to elude her. As the rite continued, her attempts to match the style and inflection of her superior came closer and closer to the mark. So, too, did the surge of power from Anna's grip increase in strength. It flowed up through Karina's arm and wound its way around her heart, lending an invisible fire to its inner chambers, and was immediately doused by the insufficiency of her oration. She felt as if her passion was entangled in a net of sleep, her fervor like a torch reluctant to take flame, but after little more than a dozen rounds, the spark was enkindled at last. Karina could feel it in the hollow of her chest—a dancing point of light that rose and fell in time with the monotonous periodicity of the metronome.

The call and response came to a halt as Anna ceased to recite her lines. In the minutes that followed, the subtle force that flowed between them continued to feed the fire in Karina's heart, while the ticks of the metronome drove it ever upward. It rose like a serpent up the column of her spine, taking refuge in the cavity of her skull. There it seemed to shed a light which was wholly interior. The glow was as pale and soft as starlight, coating the bleak and barren landscape of her inner vision like freshly fallen snow upon a field.

Karina turned her attention back to her physical surroundings. Anna had again assumed the aspect of a sphinx, her face a veil of mystery in which her eyes were set like gleaming diamonds. She loosed her grip on the younger poet's hand, placed the match safe on the floor, and reached over to stop the pendulum from swinging. A smile slowly formed upon her face as she maintained the eye contact that had been established from the rite's inception. "I think it's safe to say that the first part of the process has proven successful," she said. "How do you feel?"

"As fraudulent as ever," responded Karina, certain that the other woman was fully aware of the impressions she'd received during the course of the procedure.

"Well, you're not a fully vested poet yet," said Anna, her manner having again given way to her usual gaiety. "The greater part of the ordeal lies yet before us." She rose, took up the metronome, and placed it back atop the bookcase where she'd found it. "You'll need to select a card," she said to Karina, who had remained upon the floor amidst the flaming candles. "Choose among the specimens that have their faces hidden. The others, having been exposed, will have lost something of their luminosity."

Karina required no time at all to make her choice. Her attention was drawn to a card that lay face-down immediately to her left. Its back side was illustrated with a mesmerizing pattern of slate-blue and gold. The labyrinth of elegant curves was arranged around two star-like formations near the top and bottom. "May I see its face?" she inquired, to which Anna made an affirmative noise as she struggled to remember precisely where she'd originally found the wooden die. Karina turned the card over to behold the nine of clubs. Sparrows with gray and white feathers perched upon three of the ebony icons.

The candles were snuffed and the cards gathered up

and placed back inside their cloth wrapping. Anna once again joined the younger poet on the floor, sitting on the heels of her boots with her knees before her. Karina felt decidedly vulnerable, as if the secret flame of her desire had been exposed in a place that she'd long kept to herself. Anna, for her part, displayed a sensitivity and tact that was becoming of her noble bearing.

"We're not yet nearly halfway finished, I'm afraid," she said without an ounce of frivolity. It seemed so easy for her to slip into a far more serious mien than usual when she intended to convey something of importance. "It will be necessary for me to undertake a rather arduous excursion into the woods to the south of the manor. You must wait for one hour, then come after me. It's crucial to the operation that you find me, though a very definite boundary must be crossed in order to do so."

Karina felt that it would be impertinent to question precisely what was meant by the crossing of a boundary. It was clear that she'd be told what she needed to know and nothing more. If Anna were to give away too much, she somehow knew, it would invalidate the operation. "I understand," she said at last, placing herself into the hands of providence.

"Just as with the first part of the process, there are potential dangers," continued Anna. "Should you fail to locate me, there will be consequences for us both. I must warn you that these are rather dire."

"I understand," repeated Karina, after a much briefer pause.

Anna reached out a hand and placed it on the other's shoulder. There was an implication of finality in the gesture that took Karina by surprise. She was well aware that there was no reversing the stage of the process that had now been completed. It occurred to her that she may perhaps have been a little rash in her agreement to undergo an operation that she knew nothing about.

"There's a trellis that runs from one side of the balcony to the ground below," said Anna as she rose and stepped over to the double doors. "We can make use of it to leave the house directly from the office. A poet never takes the front door if she can help it." She placed one hand upon the glass as if to ascertain the temperature outside. Karina rose to join her, wishing that she could craft an appropriate epigram in response. She was still a little dazed by the sensations that had overtaken her just moments before. She craved a cigarette, though she supposed she would be afforded the opportunity to enjoy one soon enough. As soon as the thought occurred to her, she grew anxious that Anna would forbid it.

"You should try to get some rest," said the poetess as she gazed out through the glass doors toward the woods. "It's best if you don't watch me go. You need not worry about oversleeping. You'll wake in time."

"We'll see if sleep will come to me," said Karina. "It won't hurt to try, in any case."

"There's one more thing that I should tell you" said Anna, as if in afterthought. She turned halfway around to face the bookshelves, her gaze fixed on nothing at all. "You'll need to present your choice of cards at the border station. There are particular rites and codes of conduct that must be observed during your crossing. These may be intuited or deduced." She looked up once more to meet the eyes of the younger woman. "You'll find that your technique, so far as you've developed it, will be of invaluable aid to you."

Karina desperately wanted to ask precisely what would be expected of her, yet she knew she mustn't. As it was, she sensed that Anna was struggling to determine what she ought to tell her and what ought to be withheld. She wondered if the woman would wear a coat when she slipped out, or whether she'd simply brave the frigid weather in her skirt, top and boots. The latter prospect seemed not entirely inconceivable. The impression that the poetess imparted was suggestive of a creature somehow more than human. "One hour," said Anna, her eyes locked on Karina's own, "no more, no less."

"One hour," promised Karina, glancing over at a clock between two bookcases. The hands showed 1:35 a.m. It was later than she'd thought. Unable to think of anything else that needed to be said, she turned and slipped out of the room, traversing the short distance down the corridor to the guest bedroom.

The Flame

Karina sat on the edge of the bed and gazed through the windows at the bleak expanse of snow and ice. Little of significance could be seen to the north of the house. Even the road that led to the station was largely hidden from view due to the lower elevation of the property. Moments earlier, she had faintly heard what may have been the crunch of snow beneath a pair of soft leather boots. Listening for further evidence of footsteps, she heard only silence. She wasn't fully convinced that Anna had truly left the house.

Karina hadn't bothered to switch on the lamps when she came back into the bedroom. The relative darkness

187

drew her attention inward. She'd expected that the lambent flame behind her eyes would fade after a short time, yet still it shone with undiminished purity. Fleeting shadows seemed occasionally to pass before the source of the light, causing it to flicker at an uneven rate. Its wan and washed-out pallor was not dissimilar to the anemic luster of the winter landscape that was visible through the windows. She was given to the vague impression that the icy expanse had somehow found its way inside her.

She was disinclined to attempt sleep, lest she fail to awake in time. She imagined Anna waiting for her beneath the snow-covered alders for hours on end, permeated by the bitter cold and cursing her impertinence. She sat on the bed with her back against the wall and closed her eyes. The subtle fires that blazed within her were notably brighter when the outside world was shut out. There was something vaguely illicit about the phenomenon, as if the light derived its incandescence from the questionable virtues of duplicity and stealth. She felt that this was perfectly appropriate. She had long convinced herself that poets were naturally distrusted by those who had yet to cultivate an appreciation for the art. The source of the light would seem to be somewhere behind her. She couldn't quite locate it except by inference. The forms that passed before it, casting fleeting trails of shadow, were also hidden from her view. She imagined that these were sparrows, winging about within a space that had no fixed location, residing neither wholly within her or without, but rather in a third place that partook equally of both.

She opened her eyes to find the mounted raven staring down at her with gentle insistence from its place upon the cabinet. The circle of golden eyes within its breast seemed to peer straight through her and into the place from which her interior light originated. She checked the clock upon the desk. Twenty minutes had passed since Anna had presumably left the house. She felt restless and unsettled. The prospect of remaining on the bed for another two thirds of an hour was positively distasteful to her. For the most part, she preferred her own company to that of others, but at the moment she felt uneasy with her solitude.

She rose, thinking she would peruse the bookshelves downstairs until it was time for her to venture out of doors in search of the Russian poet. It occurred to her that she had never once set foot inside the walk-through closet that lay behind the writing desk. No furnishings were visible from either of the closet doorways. Even in the daytime, the darkness that so effectively concealed its interior was impervious to the light from the bedroom windows. The promise of uncovering new depths within the Stenger house, however insignificant, seduced her interest. The closet, in particular, appeared to have been hidden in plain sight, and thus demanded to be infiltrated and explored.

She stepped inside, one hand scrambling blindly in search of a light switch on the inner wall. Finding nothing, she switched on one of the lamps above the writing desk. This merely served, by contrast, to further obscure the space, making the already impenetrable darkness more opaque. She sought in vain for a switch on the wall behind the opposing doorway near the windows. At last, she gave in and retrieved a match from her handbag.

She bore the tiny light as if it were a torch as she ventured into the unexplored space. The ambient glow revealed an entirely empty enclosure, save for a slender wooden table that stood pressed up against the wall directly opposite the desk on the other side. She touched the flaming match head to the blackened wick of a tall white candle that had been centered on the table's surface. As the circle of light expanded, it illuminated the details of a number of additional items, many of which were crowded around the base of the candlestick. Chief among them was a photograph, turned yellow with age, which had been pinned to the wall behind the flame. An expansive chamber overflowing with sumptuous décor was shown within its thin white borders, the confines of the room extending beyond the leftmost edge of the picture. Hanging carpets and built-in cabinets covered every inch of wall space, while the wooden floor was bare except for a low stand near the center and several glowing lamps which had been arranged with no discernable order. The surface of the stand was cluttered with an assortment of unidentifiable objects. White blossoms could be seen rising from a pair of vases placed amidst the general mélange.

It took Karina a moment to realize that the room shown in the photograph was inhabited. A woman stood against the rightmost wall, her back pressed up against a door as if attempting to conceal her presence. Both hands were pressed flat against the painted surface behind her, while her gaze was directed to a point just beyond the camera. A head of thick, dark hair framed an expression which set Karina's curiosity alight; a provocative gaze tainted with unquenchable desire. It was difficult to tell, especially given the washed-out quality of the photograph, but the woman seemed inclined to something wholly other than the carnal. That she was of Chinese ancestry was nearly certain. Indeed, the entire space appeared most definitely

Asian. The designs on the carpets and the style of the lamps gave away their Eastern origins.

The remaining objects found upon the wooden table seemed designed to exalt the woman in the photograph: a short glass filled with crisp white wine, an antique hand-held mirror, an egg placed in the center of a wooden dish, a watch face, a foreign coin, and an opened package of cigarettes decorated with unfamiliar characters. Karina struggled to understand precisely what it was she'd found. It seemed to comprise a sort of offering, and yet the woman in the photograph could hardly be an ancestor of the Stengers. She could almost imagine them finding the image by chance in an antique piece of furniture, and being inspired not only to keep it but to revere the woman who occupied the chamber as a god. She found herself inexorably drawn to the unsettling figure. The woman was suffused with precisely the type of mystery that she'd long attempted to express through her poetry. She wanted to tilt the candle toward the image so that she might examine it in better light, yet she didn't dare to touch it. It seemed to her as if the woman was a patron saint of the poetic craft, having drawn her to this wayward shrine that she might impart her blessing on the trial to come. For a reason that she could never quite explain, Karina had always imagined that the art had its origin in the East.

She stood for a long moment in adoration of the woman. At length, she fell to one knee, bowed her head, and laid the fingers of one hand upon the table before the flaming candle. Upon rising, she felt somewhat silly. What would her hosts think, she wondered, were they to walk in and find her bowed in reverence before their hidden art piece? What would they think, for that matter, of their guests fleeing the sanctity of their house in the middle of the night to go cavorting in the snow under a perfectly arbitrary conceit? Gazing once more upon the photograph, she snuffed the candle and took herself back into the bedroom.

Another twenty minutes had been consumed. Karina's desire for a cigarette renewed itself with the vigor of an agitated demagogue. She was unable to ascertain whether the luminosity that persisted within the cavern of her skull had grown, or whether it had merely been momentarily overshadowed by the candlelight. She supposed she'd better fetch her winter coat, her silken scarf, and her heavy black boots. To that end, she stepped out through the bedroom door and took herself downstairs, passing again between the twin statues. The bulbs above their heads seem to glow with greater fervor than before, as if to display the piety of ancient priestesses who've lost themselves within the magnitude of their devotion. The secrets that they bore between them mirrored those that had so recently passed between the elder poet and herself, though the women depicted in the statues were clearly equals, while it hardly seemed possible that she could ever attain to Anna's stature as a poet.

Karina was surprised to find that the cigarette she'd left in the niche before the doorway had vanished. Had Lena or Konrad taken it, she wondered, or had it simply rolled off onto the floor, and from there into some unseen crevice? The parrot, whose petrified body occupied the niche, maintained an obstinate silence. The rubies in its eyes gleamed with malicious splendor in the light of the lamps above. Perhaps the ravenous bird had consumed the cigarette, butt and all. Its innards must have been removed during the mounting process. That the parrot was at least partially filled with tobacco was not entirely beyond the realm of possibility. Once Karina was properly attired, she took care to unlock the front door. She thought it wise to allow for re-entry using the time-honored method in case the trellis turned out to be too frail to hold her weight.

Precisely thirteen minutes and a half were spent sitting on the edge of the bed back up in the guest room. Karina gazed through one of the windows at the untarnished blanket of lustrous cobalt that concealed the surface of the Earth. The snow had begun to fall again. The last remnants of her patience had nearly dwindled down to nothing. She would not allow herself to leave a minute before the official mark had passed. She half expected to breach the upstairs office to only find Anna asleep in the fold-out bed, having somehow restored the cantankerous device to the center of the room without a whisper from its unwieldy metal rods. When the time came, she was relieved to find that the room had indeed been vacated, the bed still residing against the bookshelves opposite the balcony. Trusting that the elder poet awaited her in the woods, she lost no time in making her escape. She passed through the balcony door and into the stinging winter air, creeping down the trellis like a thief escaping from a house of God. Having safely made her way down, she set out into the desolate night, following the trail marked out by Anna's perfectly formed boot prints.

Thick flakes of frozen ivory assaulted the earth in unending droves, gleaming in the night air like stars fallen from their mansions in the heavens. As Karina had expected, it was much harder to ascend the southern slope that rose before the chateau than it had been to make the initial journey down the northern side. Her boots proved woefully inadequate to the task. Their soles had been made smooth by several years of overuse. She advanced toward the top of the hill with no small measure of caution, slowly drifting toward the embrace of the alders that offered their contorted limbs to the sky as if in prayer to the incoming deluge.

By the time the ground had levelled out, she was more than ready for her long-awaited cigarette. She fished the pack out of an inner pocket of her overcoat, having left all else behind except the playing card she'd chosen in the office. She'd considered taking her book of poems along with her into the woods. She might carry it as a fetish, or a symbolic link to her identity as a poet. In the end, a nagging intuition had cautioned her against it. Somehow, it seemed essential that she undergo the trial without the benefit of her possessions. Her cigarette, of course, was another thing entirely. As far as she was concerned, it was as much a part of nature as the snow itself.

She partook of the tobacco like a sacrament, which she supposed it was, as she made her way beneath the shelter of the overhanging branches. The absurdity of her undertaking took hold of her as she turned to look back upon the silent house. She was painfully aware that she hadn't the slightest clue what she was doing. There existed every possibility that she might lose herself in the darkness of the woods. She wondered as to the soundness of Anna's judgement, not to mention her own. It occurred to her that, having little faith in her own legitimacy, both as a poet and as an individual, she would do absolutely anything in order to win the approval of those that she admired. She clung to the faint hope that the very process that she'd undertaken might serve to redeem this defect in her character.

She turned to head into the cluster of trees before she'd entirely finished her cigarette, as if the act of smoking in their company bestowed honors and virtues not obtainable by any other means. Scattered beams of moonlight, filtered through the pregnant clouds, shone like paper lanterns in the interstices of the shadows. Karina had no difficulty passing through even the darkest patches. A pale, yet luminous flame would seem to have been kindled within the theater of her imagination. Her environment appeared within her mind's eye like the impression of a developing photograph. This, together with the vague forms occasionally illuminated by the ambient light from above, allowed her to proceed with a confident step.

She let her sense of orientation slowly fall from her as she continued. She considered it a sacrifice to the efficiency of the rite. By the time she cast the smoking stub into a rising bank of snow, she could no longer say with certainty precisely where she was. Beyond the initial line of alders she recognized sporadic clusters of beech and maple, along with the occasional white elm. The tracks left by the elder poet still intermittently appeared before her, though they followed an increasingly arduous course, leading Karina through patches of thick bush or grass, or the narrow spaces between contorted trunks. The frigid atmosphere, as well, had a bewildering effect upon her. She wasn't certain whether she was more affected by the lateness of the hour, the uncertainty with which she regarded her experience in the upstairs office, or the transfiguration that had overtaken her as a result.

The echoing cry of a hooded crow spread over the woods like a siren above the rooftops of a sleeping city. Karina paused, turned her attention inward, and found, to her slight unease, that the birds which seemed to flit from branch to branch above had their sole existence in the shadows cast inside of her. The impression given was that of an illuminated aviary which resided somewhere in the space behind the crown of her head. So poignant was the illusion that she felt that she could reach behind and touch it. She wondered if the sensation would ever go away. She supposed she could get used to it in time, though admittedly she was a little nervous at the fact that the light seemed slowly to increase in splendor as she pressed onward.

Anna's boot prints grew increasingly sparse, until at length they disappeared completely. The impartiality of the ivory floor gave no indication as to the whereabouts of the Russian poet. Karina let herself meander like a ship without a rudder, abandoning herself to the wiles of the night. She felt like a woman taken leave of her senses, and wondered, as she passed between two rows of frosted hazels, if this was not precisely the boundary that she'd been warned of.

The passage of time slipped away from her as she passed beneath an endless profusion of jeweled branches. Her senses were intoxicated by the sublimity of the starless sky as it seeped through the gaps in the foliage above. The terrain, while not exactly dangerous, was none too easy to traverse. Monotony conspired with beauty to craft a haunting procession of intricate scenes that could scarcely be distinguished from one another. Karina was halfway convinced that she was walking in wide circles.

The unmistakable glare of artificial light in the distance relieved her of the torpor that had begun to creep over her. It beckoned to her like a lighthouse amidst the torrent of falling snow, peering out between the frozen limbs of a regiment of poplars. A dismal exterior slowly revealed itself as she drew nearer. Rough patches of flaking lime-green paint covered a facade of chipped and tarnished brick. It looked as if the weight of the snow had partially collapsed the roof in one or two places. The light in question shone from a single window near one corner of the second story just below the overhanging eaves. The remaining windows were dark, their painted frames containing several squares of frosted glass.

The clearing in which the edifice appeared comprised an island in the dense woods. The poplars resumed undaunted on all sides, like soldiers forced to break formation around an immovable obstacle. She emerged from under their cover, coming face-to-face with the dilapidated brick. No windows appeared along the ground floor, nor was there any sign of an entrance. She took a step back and closed her eyes, taking a moment to examine the edifice in the mesmerizing glow of her internal vision. A host of black-winged snowfinches appeared before her inner eye. They hopped from place to place along the rooftop and on the windowsills, presumably having flown in from the interior space located infuriatingly behind her. She opened her eyes again to find not a single bird, whether on the surface of the building or in the surrounding branches.

The other side of the edifice revealed two black wooden doors atop a low stairway divided by a rail. Above, a row of four dark windows gaped out onto the sleeping forest.

Karina darted up the stairs without a moment's hesitation, eager to escape the biting cold that she'd been steadfastly ignoring over the course of the last hour. A wave of relief rushed through her like a rising flame as one of the doors swung open beneath her grasp.

The Border Station

She stepped inside and closed the door, passing from the tumultuous uniformity of the winter night into an intimate, if slightly barren foyer. The darkness would have been impenetrable but for the luminous haze of her second sight. The space was scarcely any warmer than the icy wood outside. An unattended service booth occupied the wall to one side, while an iron door and a long, low bench framed the featureless wooden floor. A rather plain, yet not displeasing chandelier hung from the high ceiling, its bulbs emitting only shadows beneath the network of winding cracks that extended from the plaster at its base. Karina scanned the walls for a light switch. Spotting one, albeit in a questionable state of repair, she stayed her hand as she realized that she could see nearly as well in the semi-darkness as she could expect to in the light.

She assumed that she'd reached the border station that Anna had spoken of earlier. Peering through the glass window before the booth, she observed a cramped little office with unpapered walls. One side was taken by a wide shelf of stained red wood, upon which several clear plastic reels of what could either be recording tape or film stock were lined up in uneven rows. Their exteriors, where they were visible, were marked with pairs of letters in red or black paint. Interspersed with these were an assortment of binders, notebooks, white folders, and loose papers. From the summit hung a dusty runner of white and amber silk, its pointed end and tassels partially concealing the contents of the uppermost shelf. The whole was surmounted by a candle holder of polished brass, a stick of pale wax reaching upward like an obelisk above its elegant sconce. Karina couldn't quite discern due to the size of the glass window, but it looked as if the ceiling was as high within the booth as it was in the room in which she stood.

She continued her inspection of the far side of the glass. Pushed up against the back wall was a narrow table that supported a short wooden mail cabinet filled with square receptacles. Roughly half of the squares were empty, while the other half displayed an incongruous assortment of trivial objects. An archaic silver key stood propped up against the side of one such box, while another contained a coil of copper wire. Directly above the wire was found a broken pair of spectacles, a crack spanning one lens from the bottom to the top and one of the arms snapped neatly off. A glass container filled with opaque fluid stood next to a stack of Chinese coins. Among the more curious of the items on display was a steel pendulum affixed to the top of one of the boxes by a length of string. Directly below the tip of the pendulum appeared a slip of paper marked with arcane symbols arranged in several concentric circles.

A black typewriter crouched before the cabinet, obscuring some of the spaces along the lowermost row. A thick white candle, partly burned down, was affixed to the upper rods by a profusion of its own melted wax. Something about the writing machine enticed Karina's attention. By some inexplicable logic that she was unable to comprehend, it seemed to offer a key to the assortment of items that resided in the hollow spaces above. As an experiment, she closed her eyes before the curious device. She was startled to see, in the light of her inner lamp, a cluster of sparrows perched upon the dusty keys and scuttling along the rim of the containing tray. The mechanism seemed to seethe and effervesce as if with an electric force. An etheric discharge, felt more than seen, gathered in a pool beneath the keys and surged like an ascending prayer toward the summit of the candle. From there, as if propelled by the unkindled flame, it rose beyond the collection of objects in the cabinet and toward the lower extreme of what appeared to be a fuse box above. Karina opened up her eyes, slightly wary of the sparrows. She was not entirely pleased to find that they inhabited a space only partially visible to her.

Her scrutiny rose to follow a thick black cord that extended outward from one side of the fuse box, continuing over to a small hole cut into the plaster of the interior wall. A piece of paper had been pinned up next to the contraption. Pairs of letters were printed in a vertical sequence in alternating red and black down one side, while the opposing side featured a black ink drawing of a hummingbird with wings extended above its slender back. Karina was given to the irrational notion that, were she but to close her eyes again, the bird might escape its prison of ink and take its place among its fellows in the building's subtle twin. As much as the thought intrigued her, she was hesitant to blink.

An oblong matchbox, slightly smaller than the one she carried with her, caught her eye below the low arched opening of the booth window. With a single well-placed finger, she turned the box around that she might examine the design that appeared upon the upper surface. So minute was the image, and so fine the stylish lines in which it was rendered, that it was difficult at first glance to make out. Several seconds' scrutiny revealed a depiction of a woman sitting on an elegant divan. She resided in a Victorian-era study, surrounded by well-stocked bookshelves and lush houseplants. Her back was rigid and her arms extended before her, their flesh concealed to the elbow beneath a pair of tight-fitting gloves. Tiny wires ran from an unseen location to the seams of the gloves near her wrists, and further to two circular patches affixed to the woman's brow. Her black eyes seemed to smolder with lascivious designs. Her lips were slightly curled as if to bear up against an overwhelming rush of pleasure. A caption appeared beneath the image, the characters so minuscule that it proved nearly impossible to read: 'The sleeper awakens to a dream of the secluded chamber.' Karina pushed the matchbox back, with all due reverence, to the place in which she'd found it.

Having satisfied herself that she'd seen everything there was to see within the service booth, she headed through the door in the far wall. The space beyond was crowded with an assembly of desks lined up in neat little rows, with the exception of a few that were significantly skewed and one which was completely overturned near the back. The expanse was divided by a series of tall wooden beams that rose from floor to ceiling, while two iron stairways on either end ascended to a metal grate giving entrance to a row of offices above. As with the foyer and the service booth, the walls were covered with chipped and tarnished paint of the same dull lime-green that adorned the outside of the building. The desks were littered with charts and diagrams, along with apparatuses and instruments of several types the likes of which Karina had not seen elsewhere. Some of them were situated in stiff black attaché cases, the insides of their open lids inset with scopes and glass tubes. Others resembled old mantle clocks encased in upright wooden boxes, their timepieces replaced with knobs and meters marked with values so small as to be all but unreadable. An assembly that resembled a sewing machine from days long passed stood propped up on a stand between two desks. Its many wheels and spindles were wound about with copper wire, while a steel rod protruded from one end in a manner that suggested an antenna.

Karina was tempted to immerse herself in a thorough exploration of the equipment. She could easily pass several days engaged in the endeavor. Her attention was particularly drawn to a metal box affixed to one of the posts, similar in style to the fuse box above the cabinet in the service booth. The two boxes were connected to one another by the thick black cord that emerged from the side of the booth, its serpentine perambulations proceeding through the hole in the wall and straight up to the ceiling. From there it found its way to the wooden post and down into the top of the box before her. With every measure of caution, she stepped forward and gently opened the outer plate. The box's interior revealed a metallic surface with a shallow, rectangular niche. Leather straps hung to either side, their ends equipped with rust-encrusted buckles. Above was a plain white button and a small, square plastic window. Two faded letters printed onto strips of paper were displayed behind the latter, the 'F' following the 'J' like a somnambulist with head bowed low and both arms stretched out before him.

Reaching one hand into her inside pocket, Karina retrieved the playing card that she'd chosen earlier, holding it before her for a moment as she examined its dimensions. She would have been somewhat disappointed, as she pressed it into the niche, had it not comprised a perfect fit. With a deft hand she fastened the straps to keep the nine of clubs in place. The three buckles were located on alternating sides, forming an irregular pattern in combination with the sparrows that were distributed across the face of the card. A press of the button gave rise to a frenzy of movement behind the little plastic window. The strips of paper must have been pasted onto the outer surfaces of two wheels which had been given a lackluster spin as the button was engaged. Within seconds, the disc on the left-hand side had clicked into place, the paper affixed to its surface displaying the letter 'L' in a generic font. A moment later the second followed with so faded an 'N' that it was difficult at first glance to distinguish from an 'H'. Karina considered herself lucky that the wheels still functioned at all, given the apparent antiquity of the machine.

Vaguely amused by the feeble performance of the device, she stood and gazed for a short time upon the talismanic object that had been strapped to its surface. In the course of only a couple of hours, she'd seen and done things that ought conclusively to have proven the veracity of Anna's statements. At the very least, she'd passed beyond her previous understanding of the poetic craft, and yet she couldn't help but hold to the unreasonable notion that the rite which had taken place between herself and

Anna was purely fanciful and arbitrary, that she'd simply chanced to wander into a long forsaken office building filled with antiquated and unfamiliar equipment, that the light that she bore within her owed more to her enthusiasm and to an overactive imagination than to anything strictly real. Her skepticism existed side by side with the uneasiness that attended her newfound source of illumination. The only reasonable course of action, she decided, was simply to embrace the ambiguities that faced her and continue onward. She felt certain that her work in the desolate building was not yet finished.

She raised a hand to the surface of the machine and ran a finger along one of the buckles. The top of the central club peered like a partially concealed spy above the ragged edge of the central strap. The birds shown on the card had entirely escaped confinement, their bodies occupying the spaces between the strips of leather. She closed her eyes and was shocked nearly to death. Not only was her hand invisible to her in the light of her second sight, but a mass of small brown warblers hopped and preened themselves in the precise space in which her fingers resided. With a short, sharp cry, she flung herself back from the wooden post and onto the surface of one of the desks. She gripped the edge of the desktop with numb fingers, eyes opened wide, as every muscle in her body tensed. The thought of the pernicious birds occupying the same space as herself gave rise to a degree of anxiety that she was not at the moment prepared to accept. Rather than dwell on it, she pushed the experience violently from her mind and quickly fished her cigarettes from the pocket of her overcoat. Within seconds she'd taken herself to one of the stairways, cigarette in hand, and began to make her way through the stagnant air to the upper level of the building. She'd intended to close the metal hatch, but the damned thing could rot on its hinges for all she cared.

She was perplexed, upon reaching the level of the unlit lamps that hung from the ceiling, to find the office at the far end shrouded in darkness. It was from this space, if she was not mistaken, that she'd first noticed the light as she approached the clearing in the woods. So taken had she been with the assortment of devices on the lower floor that she hadn't noticed the lack of illumination above. She crept into the modest chamber like a prisoner escaping back into her cell. She was further surprised to find the space entirely lacking an outer window. She wondered if another room was concealed behind this one. Perhaps there existed an additional row of office suites accessible through one of the other spaces.

The light that Karina carried within her shone bright enough to penetrate the shadows in the secluded space. The increased darkness made it impossible to ignore the tiny birds that appeared within the aureole of her visionary fire. They perched upon the furnishings and gathered in small groups in the corners of the room. As tempted as she was to simply turn around and walk back out, she rather feared the consequences of failing to complete the task that lay before her. If there was any shred of hope that her unnerving condition might be resolved, it would be found only in pushing onward. She allowed herself to indulge in the familiar pleasure of her cigarette as she carefully examined the features of her new environment.

One side of the office was dominated by a wooden desk that supported a familiar device. A reel-to-reel tape player, of a type once coveted by a particular type of audiophile from her parent's generation, stood upright between two modest candelabra. Next to the desk stood a tall metal cabinet with glass doors, its inner shelves stocked abundantly with plastic reels. Karina couldn't help but notice that the machine had not been loaded with a supply reel. It was most certainly an older model, equipped with a small amplifier which ran along one side. Eager for the opportunity to dim her second sight by way of contrast, she retrieved the box of matches from her inside pocket and lit the slim white tapers that rose from the candle holders.

Three sheets of paper, nearly crumbling with age, had been pinned to the wall above the antiquated device. As with the page above the cabinet in the booth below, these were divided into two sections. On the left of each appeared a different sequence of letter pairs, while the right-hand sides were occupied with fanciful illustrations of birds. The first displayed a woodpecker, the second a swallow, while the third was decorated with what appeared to be a kingfisher, all rendered with a resourceful combination of elegant curves and crosshatches in flat black ink. A brief inspection revealed that the letters displayed on the box downstairs were nowhere to be found among the pairs of characters.

The remaining walls were inundated with blueprints held in place with masking tape, shelves stocked with thick technical manuals, a hanging cabinet filled with rust and fetid air, and elaborate arrangements of chipped and flaking paint, all of which Karina decided that she could safely ignore for the time being. The single additional element that caught her eye was a small circular opening in the lower section of the wall opposite the door. If, as she'd suspected, the lighted room lay on the far side of the wall, then some evidence of that light should be visible through the aperture, yet a brief investigation revealed nothing more than a narrow concrete tunnel that disappeared into the darkness.

By far the most enticing item in the office was the tape player. Though not a single knob or button on the face of the device was labelled, it was not difficult to comprehend the basic principles of its operation. Having stubbed the remains of her cigarette directly onto the surface of the wooden desk, she opened the glass doors of the cabinet and searched through the plastic reels inside. It didn't take her long to find the reel marked 'LN'. With every measure of care, she affixed the reel to the device upon the desk and threaded the tape through to the take-up reel on the other side. She switched the knob on the far right of the machine into what she supposed was the play position and gently raised her hands before her with her index fingers pressed against her lips. The ensuing silence sanctified the musty air like a cloud of fragrant incense smoke. Within seconds its pleasurable influence was dispelled as a rich metallic utterance began to issue forth from the speaker through a dissonant hiss of background noise. For a moment, Karina thought that the voice belonged to Anna, but a careful listen revealed that, though it was unquestionably a woman's voice, the pitch and timbre, as well as the articulation, were notably different from that of the Russian poet. The woman's delivery resembled that of an incantation.

Karina let the words drift over her, allowing the rhythm and meter of the spoken phrases to entice her ear. It could not be doubted that what she was listening to was poetry, yet she could also discern brief segments of instruction, lamentation, rhetoric, prayer, narrative, analysis, and reprimand. At times, the words appeared to comprise a catalog of terms or principles, while at others they proceeded like a paean. With each verse, the light within her intensified as if inflamed, growing steadily in both brightness and scope as the reels slowly rotated. Just as this phenomenon began to trigger her alarm, she became cognizant of a sense of familiarity that accompanied the voice. She could almost swear she'd heard the piece before, yet she couldn't put her finger on exactly where. She noted themes and motifs which were strikingly redolent of the best among the symbolist poets, rhythmic structures and evocative turns of phrase that may well have appeared within the works of Breton or Louis Aragon. A smattering of Rilke emerged from the rich verbosity. Hölderlin and Tsvetaeva would seem either to have left their influence upon the stanzas or derived their own styles therefrom. She could even detect a hint of her own work, yet the lyricism and imagery was far more developed than anything that she was capable of crafting. As she listened, never daring to switch off the tape machine, her inner radiance continued to expand. Within a couple of minutes, the light of the candles had been entirely eclipsed. The confines of the office shone as bright as day.

For the first time since she'd agreed to undergo the operation, she felt a potent sting of genuine regret. As much as she was enthralled by the mysterious voice, she was afraid that the light that afflicted her would only continue to increase. She imagined her condition escalating to the point that she could no longer manage her worldly affairs. As it was, her physical eyesight was overwhelmed by the visionary light. The birds that traversed the surface of the writing desk appeared as real to her as the desk itself. She imagined herself in a catatonic state, entirely immersed in a delusional landscape from which she was unable to emerge. A surge of panic arose within her breast as the light rose up and overflowed its bounds. It broke forth like a hallucinatory tide which threatened to sweep her up in an irresistible current. Afraid that she might drown within this radiance, Karina frantically tried to fight its advance. So overpowering were the luminous waters that she quickly gave up, allowing them to subsume her senses like a miserable candle flame overshadowed by the immensity of the sun. For but a single instant, at the moment of surrender, she ceased to exist. Her nullification was abruptly reversed as the torch that flamed within her seemed to invert itself, allowing the excess of light to disperse to some mysterious location that lay outside of the limits of her vision.

Two things transpired as this took place, both of them sufficing to draw her attention sharply back to her outer environment. The strip of tape snapped in two midway between the reels, bringing the reading to a halt even as the machine remained in operation; and a throng of small dark sparrows shot out from the opening in the bottom of the far wall. The birds poured forth like a fountain, flitting to the extremes of the room and out through the doorway in a frenzied burst of flight. Karina was engulfed within the furious exodus. She fell back against the bookshelves behind her, throwing her hands to her face to protect herself from the continual brush of wings and feathers. After the brief outpouring had subsided, she allowed herself to peer between her fingers. A few straggling specimens still poked their heads out of the small hole in the plaster, gingerly venturing onto the comparatively wide expanse of the office floor. Those among them that remained gathered in groups upon the desk and on the edges of the cabinet shelves.

Despite the disquieting flurry of activity, Karina was greatly relieved to find that the light within her had again reduced itself to a reasonable level of intensity. The sparrows continued to put her on edge, yet their presence in the flesh was far preferable to the ghostly residence that they'd maintained within her subtle vision. After a moment's hesitation, she again closed her eyes. She was hardly surprised to find that, though the walls and furnishings remained plainly visible, the sparrows that appeared before her physical eye were entirely absent in the pale internal light. Further, the light itself seemed no longer to be located behind her. Though she still couldn't quite discern its source, it would appear to have been turned to illuminate the very space that it had previously occupied. This space revealed a generous chamber carved from golden alabaster, quite free now of birds, having a high, domed ceiling with a small, circular window near the apex of the dome. A further room could just be seen on the far side of the window, in which long shadows passed back and forth near to the ceiling. They flickered and distorted in rapid formations as if illuminated by candlelight from below. Though she'd never before set eyes on the locale, it was as familiar to her as the skin upon her fingertips. All the same, she bore a trace of apprehension regarding the unseen figures whose activities were concealed in the space above.

Not entirely ready to head back out into the winter night, Karina took the opportunity to indulge in another cigarette. She put out the candles and stepped out of the office onto the metal grate. Sparrows gathered in small groups along the outer rail, occasionally venturing through a doorway or across the gulf to one of the windowsills on the further side of the building. She let herself sink down to the surface of the upper ledge, leaning back against the painted plaster that comprised the back wall. She placed the cigarette between her lips such that it rose into the air above her like a flaming tower. The excess tension slowly drained from her as she thus stared at the ceiling. She remained so for several minutes, luxuriating in the sweet tobacco as if it were the medicine of metals.

A brief exploration of the remaining office spaces revealed a collection of weathered mannequins. Very few of them were clothed, and many of them suffered from missing limbs, disjointed sockets, and broken fingers. Her first sight of them found them lying supine in a disorganized huddle on a wooden pallet. Upon investigating further, she encountered several of the wax figures propped up in chairs or seated behind writing desks. The final suite was home to a pair of dubious characters positioned before a blackboard that nearly covered one of the walls, its surface inelegantly decorated with glyphs and ciphers. One of the figures clutched a piece of chalk between his stiff and lifeless fingers, while the other had turned his back on the first, gazing as with a pensive regard through the single window that looked out onto the woods behind the building.

Before her cigarette was spent, Karina took herself downstairs and gently closed the hatch of the metal box in which her choice of cards had been secured. She sat down in one of the wooden chairs that were arranged before the desks, ignoring the contraption that occupied the surface before her. With an assiduity born of discretion, she avoided giving too much thought to the meaning of her experience in the corner office. She would have plenty of time for reflection later. For the moment, she was inclined to simply allow herself a moment of repose. She knew that there was more yet to be done. The prospect of finding the Russian poetess in the snow-filled landscape was far from certain. She shuddered at the thought of returning to her guest room without having completed her task. It seemed unlikely that Anna would allow herself to freeze to death if left unattended throughout the night, yet the potential consequences of failure were unnerving at the very least. She rose, allowed herself a final pull from the dwindling remains of her cigarette, cast the butt onto the floor, and headed back out into the icy embrace of night.

The Reliquary

Karina emerged from the border station like a leaf borne up on a capricious wind, slipping into the winter woods as if she were a fugitive. Several sparrows rushed out after her, exulting in the merciless chill of the night air as they headed for the shelter of the elms. Again, she proceeded with no direction in mind, content to take herself wherever providence might lead her. She seemed to wander through a temple carved from exquisite diamond, the thick snowfall producing the impression of an intricate labyrinth at once monotonous and holy.

If the light she bore within her had seemed illicit back in the chateau, it seemed positively scandalous now as she made her way between the naked trunks and branches.

She was complicit, she understood, in a transaction that was in no way condoned by the society in which she lived. The process had impressed itself upon her like the mark of Cain. Though this was bound to lead to disadvantages in certain areas of her life, there was little question as to whether or not the trouble would be worth it.

At length, the alders in their masses began to grow sparser, parting company with one another to give way to wide expanses of barren snow. Desecrated artifacts of brick and stone began to pass by with increasing frequency. A bell tower emerged from the frozen earth, its cap rising high into the tenuous domain of the night air. The entire structure leaned at a portentous angle, giving rise to the impression that it might collapse at any moment. While the belfry had been broken in half, exposing the bell chamber to the scrutiny of the impetuous sky, the bell itself had managed to remain intact. It softly vibrated as the wind caressed its surface, moaning like a wounded animal abandoned by its pack.

A little further on was found a ruined stairway. The cracked and blistered stones ascended several stories above Karina's head before abruptly coming to an end. A magnificent willow cowered in its shadow, its drooping branches inundated with great clots of crystal powder. She considered scaling the heights that she might be afforded a bird's-eye view of the surrounding area, but was dissuaded by the decrepit condition of the structure.

The remains of several sections of standing wall were found as well within the near vicinity. The fortifications were arranged according to an inexplicable plan, each section laid out at right angles to its neighboring fragments. Some of these were solid, while others harbored narrow archways. Karina wondered precisely what it was that had once occupied this place. What remained of the architecture suggested a labyrinthine complex that rose far above the surface of the earth.

As she explored, she gradually noticed that the wail from the nearby bell tower was joined by a host of other sounds: a barely discernable lamentation which seemed to come from far beneath her feet, several high-pitched drones whose origin was largely obscured by the soft howl of the wind, the distant modulations of what almost sounded like a church choir. She stood in place and closed her eyes, an effort which revealed nothing but the domed chamber of white stone that still rose behind her. A single shadow fell across the windowsill above, faintly shimmering as if affected by the wind that caressed her brow. A seemingly endless expanse of pallid light extended before her, with no trace of a horizon in the distance. Returning again to her physical environment, she was given to an unexpected certainty that Anna was nearby. Traces of the woman's character seemed to permeate the surrounding ruins. Even the empty spaces beneath the arches bore the tenuous mark of her influence. Karina was reminded of the sense of intimacy that they'd shared in Konrad's office. She understood that something of the Russian poet was now a part of her. Whatever it was that had passed between them had not escaped the imprint of the hands that had administered the rite.

Continuing on, she passed beneath a tall archway flanked by two smaller side doors and into a space that may once have been a courtyard. The surrounding walls had long since been reduced to broken chunks, the rough boundary that remained occasionally giving way to more dignified stretches of undiminished stone. On the far side of the open area arose an arch of similar size to the one through which she'd just passed, the fallen capstone lying buried below beneath a thick veneer of snow. Her advance was halted by the unambiguous sensation of the near presence of another. Slowly, and with all due caution, she pivoted in place. Her heart was flushed with anticipation, yet her body remained braced for conflict.

There stood Anna, black as pitch, her petrified body leaning against one side of a shallow niche like a statue that had been propped up against a temple wall. Her skin and clothing were coarse and grained, as if she'd been fashioned from charcoal. There could be no doubt that it was she, despite the transformation which had overtaken her. The presence and bearing of the Russian poetess, in all of her stately grandeur, occupied the substance of the harsh mineral figure like a god in a stone idol. One arm was held before her, palm raised and fingers slightly splayed as if to confer a benediction on the fallen snow. Her eyes, like unmoving stones of obsidian, gazed over Karina's shoulder and into the emptiness that lay beyond. Low candles flamed in smaller niches that occupied the wall to either side.

Karina approached her mentor in silence, hardly expecting that words might pass between them while she was in her current state. With the exception of her own conspicuous tracks, she noticed that the snow before the depression in which the poet resided was unmarked. She raised one hand and let her fingers interlace with those of the older woman. The sensation of the rough material upon her skin unsettled her a little, abraded as her hands had already become due to their prolonged exposure to the freezing cold. Flakes of Anna's particulate flesh rubbed off on her own. Already her fingers were stained black by their contact with the chalky substance. Her attention was soon distracted by a decidedly magnetic pull that seemed to emanate from the center of the woman's palm. The light that dwelled within her skull, which had grown noticeably brighter in the presence of the poet, was thus pulled swiftly downward. It emitted a soft pulse as it passed through her throat, giving rise to a delicate surge of pleasure as its radiance engulfed her collarbone. Its descent was halted upon reaching the space behind her sternum. There it seemed to settle into place, emitting a gentle click which softly resounded through the dispassionate night air.

Karina again withdrew her hand, her scrutiny directed to a space which occupied the tiny region between her breast and the small of her back. There, in the light of her internal fire, she beheld a treasure house of strange antiquities, a reliquary filled with curios and remnants that were not entirely her own. Her breath caressed the fragments of a lost empire, the ruins of which she was unquestionably heir to. She felt as if she'd joined the ranks of an invisible tradition whose titles and principles had been expunged from all official records. She was left with not a trace of doubt that the second and final phase of the operation had been successfully completed.

She gazed once more upon the immobile face of her instructress, curious as to whether Anna would be waiting for her when she returned to the chateau. She suspected it highly likely. The woman was possessed of a cleverness and tenacity that far surpassed her own. Karina doubted that they would speak of the procedure, now or in the time to come. She considered the near certainty that she herself would be required, in turn and for some other fledgling poet, to assume the role that Anna had fulfilled for her. The thought gave rise to a certain apprehension. The older woman stood before her, transfigured and without heat, a hollow shell for forces and powers for which she had no name or context. She couldn't begin to imagine what it must be like to abide in that state, nor how exactly the transition might be accomplished. She could only assume that a greater understanding of the rite would come to her as she continued to refine her craft. She supposed that she need not worry about the eventuality for the time being. With a final glance upon the blackened body of the Russian poet, she stepped away and took herself back through the archway.

The eastern horizon was obscured by the dark trunks of the alders which rose like living pylons in the distance. Karina doubted that the first rays of the sun had yet begun to breach the horizon. She dutifully followed the trail of her boot prints through the snow, only the slightest bit concerned that she might find her tracks obscured as she drew closer to the Stenger house. The journey back would take at least a couple of hours. The prospect of enjoying even a minimal amount of sleep before the onset of the coming day was laughable at best. As she passed the bell tower once more, its resonant howl having considerably diminished, she contemplated the precise influence that her ordeal would exert upon her future verse. Would her work grow in time to be as eloquent as that of her benefactor's? She knew that she must ultimately establish a style all her own. If poetry, as Anna had suggested, was truly defined by an act of concealment, then she supposed the hiding of the light within her would be sufficient to arouse the muse. The snowfall began to pick up again as Karina approached the first line of naked alders. She slipped between their frozen embraces as if in flight from the promise of the coming dawn.

A PARTIAL LIST OF SNUGGLY BOOKS

Lightning Source UK Ltd.
Milton Keynes UK
UKHW010947201120
373762UK00003B/558

9 781943 813391